Love, Lies & Consequences trilogy

Book Two : Lies

By

Susan Elle

For

Ursula Publishing UK

Love, Lies & Consequences
Book Two : Lies
Text Copyright © 2013
By Susan Elle
Ursula Publishing UK
All Rights Reserved.

Cover Photograph
© Yuri Arcurs/Dreamstime.com

ISBN 978-1-910753-06-4

Other Books by Susan Elle

The Sara Colson Trilogy includes
Sara's Child
Sara's Loss
Sara's Shame
All the above also available as audio books.

Catherine Colson-Sayers Investigations
CCS Investigations : Bk 1 : Missing
CCS Investigations : Bk 2 : The Chosen
CCS Investigations : Bk 3 : Travis
CCS Investigations : Bk 4 : Deleted
CCS Investigations : Bk 5 : Mind Games, due out end
Aug 2015, twice the length of previous books.

Tempest
Broken

Love, Lies & Consequences Trilogy
Love : Bk1
Lies : Bk2
Consequences : Bk3

Langdon Trilogy
Heart & Home : Bk1
Heart of a Lion : Bk2
Heart of Stone : Bk3
www.susan-elle.com

Table of Contents

PROLOGUE

Douglas Benson walks to the hall where his daughter's wedding service is due to begin and hesitates outside of its large double doors.

Dressed in his 'father of the bride' suit, he straightens his jacket and tie then takes a deep breath.

"Jesus-H-Christ, this has got to be one of the hardest roles I've ever had to play. No lines, no rehearsals, just walk out there and hope they don't lynch me!"

Taking hold of the large brass handles, he opens the doors wide and makes the walk down the aisle solo, that he should have been making with his new-found daughter on his arm.

All eyes turn to him, and then the hum of wagging tongues begins to build.

Ignoring the curious frowns aimed at him, Douglas strides purposefully to the front of the room.

He goes first to Palmer Johnson, who is looking confused and pale. Douglas puts his mouth close to the groom's ear then stands back to stare daggers into Palmer's stunned blue eyes.

Turning to the buzzing crowd, Douglas reins in his temper and delivers the bad news.

CHAPTER ONE

"I just don't understand," Dorothy Johnson tells Palmer as they sit together in her lounge. "This isn't like Zoe at all. She wouldn't have run away without good reason!"

Holding out the letter he'd found on the dressing-table next to a bunch of flowers that had been delivered earlier that day to Zoe's suite, Palmer doesn't answer, he can't!

"What is this rubbish!?" Dorothy demands, getting to her feet and handing the letter to her husband to read.

"She's been getting them for a while now," Palmer explains. "Each one worse than the last...but I never thought she would believe them. I was wrong..."

With his head in his hands, Palmer visualises the

words of the note, recalling them perfectly as he's already read it a dozen times and more.

'I warned you over and over again, but you just wouldn't believe me. Now see for yourself, bitch!'

"What exactly does this mean, son?" Bill Johnson frowns angrily down at the note in his hand.

"I'm not sure; there was nothing else with the note so I can only assume that Zoe took something with her – something that supposedly proved what these letters have been accusing me of." Palmer pushes both hands back through his dishevelled hair again, squeezing it tight at the roots. "Aaaah!" he yells in angry frustration. "We talked about this. She said she believed me, that she was happy to be getting married. She lied!"

"No!" Dorothy moves to stand over her bereft son and puts a hand on his shoulder. "No, Palmer, I don't believe she did. Whatever came with this note was obviously convincing – I think you'll find that Zoe is suffering just as much as you are right now."

He lifts his eyes to his mother's kind face and nods. "You could be right." He stands, looking around at Connor and Laura. "Did she say anything to either of you?"

"We weren't best buddies," Connor volunteers, "so I doubt I came close to being on her confidant list."

"But you would have," Palmer turns to a tearful Laura.

"You were good friends — if she had a confidante it should have been you!"

Paling visibly, Laura looks around to see all eyes turned in her direction. "But she didn't tell me anything," she squeaks, then bursts in to another fit of crying.

Connor looks daggers at Palmer, "Leave her alone, damn it! Isn't upsetting one woman enough for you?!"

Squaring up to his younger brother, Palmer glares at him eye to eye. "I did not do anything to upset Zoe! For the last time, these letters are all lies!"

"Yeah, well obviously Zoe didn't think so!" And with that, Connor puts a hand under Laura's elbow and escorts her from the house.

Once seated in his car, Connor turns to Laura and grins brightly. "You were brilliant, babe! Abso-fucking-lutely brilliant!"

But Laura just continues to cry, sobbing into the handkerchief that Bill had given to her.

"Oh for fuck's sake stop with the water-works!" Connor turns in his seat and starts the car with a loud rev of the engine. "We did it! You and me, we fucking did it! Now let's see how 'the big man' likes his just deserts! I hope he chokes on them!"

"Take me home, Connor," Laura pleads between soft sobs. "I just want to go home."

"I just want to go home," Connor mimics cruelly. "Well that's fine by me – I've got things to do and people to see!"

"I can't believe I let you talk me into this," Laura bites back, her anger at Connor finally giving her some backbone.

"You saw the photos," he sneers. "Palmer is not the innocent he makes himself out to be. Now everyone knows it!"

"I know I saw the photos, but Palmer never acted like that kind of man – like he'd play around on Zoe like that!"

"Exactly! He pulled the wool over everyone's eyes," Connor laughs scathingly. "All these years I've been told to be more like my sainted brother. Well now they'll change their tune. My parents will look at me differently now!"

"Is that what this has been all about?" Laura asks.

"Part of it, sure! I'm sick of being told how much better my brother is than me. 'Why can't you be more like Palmer' 'Why didn't you invest your money like Palmer' or 'When will you learn from your brother, he's done so well for himself'" Connor glares out of the windscreen and screeches the car round a nasty bend.

"Well I'm sick of hearing about how great my brother is – now they'll look at him differently, too!"

Having dropped Laura off at her parent's house, Connor drives over to Zoe's and parks his car a little way down the road and waits.

Four hours later he's still waiting. Zoe hasn't been back to her mother's house and there hasn't been any sign of movement inside.

Is she still at the hotel? Is she hiding out in one of the other rooms?

No point going back over there now. No, I'll just wait here until she shows up, then I'll make my move.

It's pitch black, not even a star to light the shadows, and Connor is still waiting for Zoe to arrive home.

"Where the fuck is she? It's bloody midnight, where the bloody hell is she?"

Thumping the steering wheel, Connor forces himself to calm down. He doesn't want to look angry when he moves in to comfort the bride that wasn't!

He's gone over and over his lines. He'll offer his commiserations, be full of disgust over his brother's despicable behaviour and offer to help in any way he can.

"Yes, in time she'll turn to me and I'll be right there waiting to pick up the pieces of her broken heart," he laughs out loud.

But by 8 o'clock in the morning, Zoe still hasn't arrived home.

At 8:35 Carly Benson arrives home, driven by none other than Craig Stanley.

Connor watches her get out of the car and can see how distraught the woman is.

And there's good old Craig doing his knight in shining armour act. You make me sick! Just another suck-up to Palmer, another worshiper at the feet of 'the big man'!

Well, how the mighty have fallen! Now we'll see just how far down he can go.

For a week, Connor spends every waking hour outside of Zoe's house waiting for her to come back home. And the longer he waits the more his obsession grows.

Her mother comes and goes as normal, but Zoe is nowhere to be seen.

Damn it! You can't have fallen off the face of the earth! Where the fuck are you?

Eventually, Connor has to get help – he's desperate to find Zoe and will do so at any cost.

The detective agency he puts on the case has an excellent reputation, but it costs a small fortune.

Time to make some money – and not the peanuts he earns working for his brother.

So long, Bro, time for Connor Johnson to step out of your shadow!

CHAPTER TWO

Henry Snelson is the 60 something owner of a construction company that has lost out to Palmer Johnson too many times of late.

Waiting in the lounge of an out of the way hotel, he wonders what exactly Palmer's little brother is up to. He'd requested this meeting, suggesting that it would be beneficial to both of them.

Watching the younger Johnson boy walk into the lounge, Henry narrows his piggy eyes even more than they already are as he watches him approach.

Henry doesn't get up but waves a hand to a nearby seat.

"Henry," Connor smiles and takes his seat, "good to see you. Thanks for meeting me."

"Let's cut to the chase," Henry finishes off his neat brandy and puts the empty glass down in front of Connor. "You refill that with a double brandy and then you can tell me what the hell it is you want!"

Connor just looks deadpan back at the paunchy man and feels his stomach turn over. Not with fear, but with disgust.

"You're going to be putting your hand deeper in your own pocket than it takes to buy your own drinks," Connor tells him quietly. Firmly. Not taking his eyes off Snelson for a second.

Snelson's top lip curls but he waves over to a waiter and places his order, and when the waiter looks to Connor he nods his head for him to add his own drink to it.

"Now what the hell is this all about, I'm a busy man?!"

Leaning back in his chair, Connor finds that he's enjoying himself. "Not as busy as you'd like to be. In fact..." he pulls himself more upright "...I hear business is bad. Palmer seems to be outbidding you more often than not."

Snelson's cheeks burn redder than usual, looking like his blood-pressure is fit to burst!

"Did you come here to gloat or to talk about something I'm actually interested in hearing?" Snelson leans forward in his seat, his piggy eyes glaring. "I don't need some snot nosed kid telling me about a business I built from the ground up over the last 20 years!"

Pursing his lips and nodding in consideration, Connor takes the drink the waiter has just proffered to him. Swirling the liquid in his glass, Connor contemplates it then looks up at Snelson.

"Then you're not interested in how this snot nosed kid can help you win more of those lucrative contracts that you've been losing out on?"

Snelson actually sounds like a pig when he snorts a laugh at Connor's suggestion. "You expect me to believe that you would sell out your own brother...?" But his expression changes when he sees the hate in Connor's eyes.

"You know what, boy, I believe you would. Yes sir, I believe you would."

"I wouldn't have wasted my own time asking for this meeting if I wasn't prepared to deliver," Connor tells him stonily. "But it won't come cheap!"

Nodding, Snelson considers the idea. "When and how?"

"You don't need to know the how, but the when is as soon as you like," Connor tells him confidently. "You tell me which contracts you're interested in and I'll supply you with a copy of Palmer's tender in time for you to pip him at the post. Good enough?"

Snelson can hardly believe his luck. Whatever this kid's brother did to him it must have been bad. "There's a new hotel complex planned for the airport – The Bickenhill Hotel. You get me a copy of his tender and I'll pay you ten grand, no questions asked."

But 'the kid' surprises him by throwing his head back and laughing long and loud. "You're a real douche-bag, do you know that?"

With his cheeks purpling with rage now, Henry Snelson makes to stand, but then reconsiders and eyes Connor warily. "You have another figure in mind?"

"Hell yes, I have another figure in mind!" Connor takes the time to finish his drink before making any further reply. "I haven't worked for my brother this long without getting to know what his take-home-pay is. You can multiply your offer by five and still make a mint. And you will, if you want a chance of getting that contract!"

Paling now, Snelson has to calm his breathing and think this through. But it doesn't take long to realise that the kid has him over a barrel. "Fifty grand then and you'll supply a full copy of your brother's tender?"

"I will," Connor nods. "I know it's just been completed so I'll get it to you in a couple of days." He leans across the small table between them and holds out his hand to Snelson. The old man takes it and the deal is sealed.

Standing, Connor looks down at Snelson, "I'll be in touch. Cash on delivery, and don't even think about a double-cross or I'll take this deal to one of your other competitors and you can watch them profit from your loss!"

The following night, instead of sitting in his car waiting for Zoe to come home, Connor drives over to Johnson Construction and uses a copy of the keys he'd talked Laura into loaning him to let himself in.

His trusting brother had already told him the alarm code and he quickly makes his way up to the 15th floor and Palmer's office.

Without turning on any lights, Connor uses a small torch to search his brother's office files. "Good old Palmer still likes to keep a paper copy of everything. Bingo!"

Pulling out the Bickenhill Hotel file, Connor takes it along the corridor to the photocopier and fires a copy off.

Making sure that everything is back in place, Connor takes his copy of Palmer's tender and locks the building up tight, remembering to reset the alarm.

Driving to the Holiday Inn off the M6 he settles himself in the bar and makes a call to Henry Snelson.

"When do you want it?" he asks without preamble.

Snelson doesn't play dumb, "As soon as you can get your greedy little mitts on it!"

Connor laughs humorously, "Now now, Snelson, let's

not start with the name calling. I can think of a few to describe your part in this too."

Letting out a disagreeable harrumph, Snelson asks, "How do I know I'm getting the only copy? You could be pulling some kind of scam, selling copies to multiple bidders!"

Sneering at his phone, despising the man at the other end of the call, Connor doesn't even bother to answer. He presses the end button and leaves the pig to sweat.

Snelson lasts precisely two minutes before returning Connors call. "I have a right to be concerned - 50 grand is a lot of money!"

"You ever call me a liar again and I'll take this tender, and any others I get my hands on, to your other big rival, Sloane Construction," he promises angrily.

"No, no, let's not be hasty here," Snelson backtracks quickly. "I have the money; we could make the exchange tonight if you've a mind?"

That was exactly what Connor had planned, but now he's tempted to keep the slug waiting. But he's going to have costs coming through from the PI he's set onto finding Zoe.

"I'm at the Holiday Inn off the M6," he tells Snelson. "Be here no later than an hour from now and bring the money."

With that he ends the call and downs the last of his whiskey. Holding the glass up to the barman, he orders a double.

Now who's rolling in dough! I'll show you, big man, and all the rest of you for writing me off! Connor Johnson has only just begun to earn big bucks. Then I'll be able show Zoe a good time and afford to give her the best of everything. She won't even look twice at Palmer by the time I'm finished!

Laura can't believe what she has done, what Connor has gotten her into. How could she have betrayed her friend?

But did I? If Palmer was cheating, and he looked like he was locking lips pretty intently with that blonde in the photos, then Zoe deserved to know. Surely I did the right thing?

But inside, Laura knows that what is troubling her is the way she went about it. The way Connor had told her to deliver the letters, anonymously. And she remembers how scared and intimidated by the letters Zoe had been.

But I knew she was safe. I knew she didn't have a stalker. Christ! I let her walk around in fear because I was too scared to tell her the truth. I'm a stupid coward and I don't deserve a friend like Zoe.

While she admits a lot of her shortcomings to herself,

Laura can't bring herself to admit that it is the man she loves who has really deceived everyone. She continues to tell herself that he was acting in Zoe's best interest. That his brother was just doing what he always had, putting on a goody-two-shoes act that fooled his parents and everyone around them, and made Connor look bad in the process.

I'm the only one who has ever stood by him – Connor told me that himself! He loves me, even if he can't say the words, I know that he loves me. I can't let him down now. It wouldn't help anyone if all this came out.

No, I'll just stay quiet and carry on like normal. No one will ever guess it was me. And it really wasn't...it was all Connor's idea! No reason for anyone to get mad at me...

Counting his money, Connor feels a glow of triumph running through his veins. "It's all here – now you can go home and do some interesting bedtime reading. I think you'll find all you need in here." And he hands Snelson a large manila folder with the Bickenhill Hotel tender in it.

"Did you find any more?" Snelson asks, his piggy eyes and puffy cheeks glowing with sweat.

He disgusted Connor, but he was a good source of easy money if he played his cards right.

"I copied a few other interesting documents while I was there," Connor tells him lazily. "I'll let you know if there's anything I think you might be interested in. Or maybe I should ask Sloane if he's interested – I'm sure he'd pay top dollar to sink you and Palmer at the same time!"

Snelson's cheeks purple instantly and his little piggy eyes manage to go round. "Don't start making threats, boy! I don't like being double crossed any more than you would!"

"Take it easy," Connor sneers, "I don't want you having a heart-attack in my car. And there's no double-cross. You've got what you paid for – if you want exclusivity it'll cost you a hell of a lot more!"

"Don't get greedy, son!"

"Greedy! You just paid me a pittance of what that information is really worth and you know it!" Stuffing the bag with the 50K in it into the back of the car, Connor turns impatiently away and starts the car, giving Snelson his cue to exit it.

"We keep this deal exclusive and I'll double your next payout," Snelson offers hopefully.

For a minute, Connor considers turning him down. He doesn't like Snelson, doesn't like the way he talks down to him.

"I'll take that into consideration when I'm weighing up my options," he tells him noncommittally.

"I'll triple it," Snelson grovels piteously.

"Jesus, I really did sell myself short," Connor laughs. "You pay me another 20K for this job and I guarantee you exclusivity on the terms you stated for anything else I get. Now I have to leave," he tells the grunting little man as he hauls his heavy frame out of Connors low slung car.

He turns back with his hand on the open door. "You've got a deal. Do I add the rest on to the next payment?"

"Yeah, sure," Connor nods nonchalantly, having had enough of this man's company. "I'll call you when I'm ready to deal again." And he revs the car engine to let Snelson know that he's getting impatient to leave.

Connor doesn't actually go anywhere. He waits for Snelson to drive away then pulls his car into a more private part of the car park and calls Laura.

"Hey, babe, want to spend the night in a swanky hotel with me?"

Having picked her up, Connor takes Laura up to the room he'd booked them into.

"So, what do you think?" he asks, opening the door to a suite of rooms that includes its own large sitting room.

"Jesus, Connor..." Laura gasps as she moves across the plush carpet, "...can you afford really afford this?"

He laughs and pulls hands full of money out of the bag he'd brought up with them.

"I can afford anything I damned well please," he boasts, then pulls her roughly into his arms. "But right now, I just want you," he tells her, and jams a hand up her skirt to finger her crotch!

She gasps with shock, but Laura loves the bad-boy side of Connor. It's what drew her to him in the first place.

His fingers push their way into her knickers and into her pussy, and she's instantly wet.

"Connor..."

The need in her voice fires his loins as Connor takes relentlessly. He doesn't bother undoing her buttons, but drags her blouse open and lifts her breasts out of her bra cups.

"You have great tits," he smiles, before dipping his head to take her nipples one by one into his mouth over and over again.

Her head falls back, and Laura can't think clearly enough to refuse his demands. Her skirt is on the floor, quickly followed by the rest of her clothes.

"Slow down," she gasps, but he doesn't take any notice. Now his head is between her legs and his tongue is ravaging her clit with urgent flicks that drive her wild.

"That's it, baby, I want you wet and wild," he tells her, right before he thrusts his tongue inside her and she goes into orgasm.

Standing, he twists them so that the oversized settee is behind him. Connor drops down onto it and pushes the lower half of his clothing off of his legs. His cock is standing to attention, thick and hard and hot.

Taking it into his hands, Connor looks at Laura, "My turn."

He doesn't need to ask twice. Laura drops to her knees between his and takes him into her mouth. She has never done this for anyone but Connor, and he hadn't really given her a choice the first time.

As far as he is concerned, what he does for her she has to do for him. And, but for the first time when he'd made her gag, Laura has actually come to like pleasuring Connor this way.

Only now she makes sure that she is in control, it is up to her how deep and fast she takes him in.

The first time had almost put her off fellating a man for life. She had been under Connor and he had fucked her mouth as roughly as he'd later fucked her pussy.

His groans drive her on now, that memory distant and almost forgotten. She loves to get Connor hot like this, and he's told her that her mouth is the most fuckable he's ever known. And that is good enough for Laura.

He is close now, and she has to decide quickly whether to swallow or stop and move to straddle him.

But Connor must have read her mind. He takes the choice away from her when his hand comes down on her head, holding her in place and he moves his hips beneath her.

Letting out a yell of satisfaction as his hot seed hits the back of her throat, Connor forces her to swallow.

Ok. Not so much in control then. But at least he didn't thrust it down my throat and half choke me!

CHAPTER THREE

Zoe sits out back of the florists and works on a simple arrangement that an old gentleman has asked her to prepare for his wife.

"It's our ruby wedding anniversary," he'd told Zoe. "These are the same flowers she carried on our wedding day – I want to show her that I still remember." And he'd smiled lovingly.

How lucky his wife is. To have a husband who would go to so much trouble to show a wife of 40 years how much he still loves her. And to remember her bouquet flowers, that must be rare. I wonder if Palmer would have remembered.

Shaking thoughts of Palmer from her mind, Zoe concentrates on the beautiful arrangement and tries not to let her mind wander.

But it is getting harder not to think of Palmer, as her pregnancy becomes more real.

I'd never have believed that morning sickness could be so relentless. And that's a joke in itself! Morning sickness – they should call it 24/7 sickness, I can't seem to keep anything down lately.

Her pregnancy had been a terrible shock to Zoe. Having run away from her wedding she had hidden out at a local hotel, courtesy of her father.

He'd been so great. Her father, a stranger who had only recently walked back into her life, had made a commitment to stay in her life for as long as she would have him. He'd vowed to make up for his shortcomings and she had allowed him back into her life with just one small proviso.

If he ever let her down she would cut him out of it without a backwards glance. And he had accepted her terms unreservedly.

Because he had been able to pay cash for the cottage, the sale had gone through in only days, with a little more cash greasing the wheels, she suspected.

She hadn't wanted to take his money, but he had insisted and she hadn't been able to think of an alternative way to get away from Palmer.

Her pregnancy hadn't been known to her then, but just a couple of weeks after moving to the cottage the morning sickness had started.

And even then I was too dumb to connect the dots. It took Tara all of two days to suss out what was wrong with me.

Picking up another white lily, she inserts it into the arrangement she's working on.

Stomach flu, huh! But then, I've never been pregnant before and Tara has two kids.

"Hey, that's coming along nicely," Tara smiles down at Zoe's work appreciatively. "You were a gift from the gods! I've had experienced florists working for me that didn't have a quarter of your natural talent!"

"Why, thank you," Zoe chuckles. "I must admit, I do love the work. I've always enjoyed creating things – my own clothes, embroidery...I even tried pottery once but my mother told me not to give up the day job when I gave her a wonky flower vase."

The two women enjoy a light-hearted laugh at Zoe's expense.

"Then I should thank her. I would have lost out big time," Tara tells her.

"I really do appreciate the work," Zoe smiles up at her boss, who is only a few years older than herself. "Not many people would have been happy to take on a pregnant single woman."

Tara pulls up a stool to sit opposite Zoe.

"You don't have to, but it might help to talk about what happened to bring you here," Tara offers quietly. "Your accent isn't one I recognise so I'm guessing you're from quite a ways away?"

Hesitating, Zoe frowns down at the arrangement and pushes another flower into place.

Tara makes to rise from her stool, but Zoe reaches a hand across to lay over Tara's.

"No, don't leave, I'm just trying to straighten out the mess in my head," Zoe tells her. "It's all so confusing. We were so in love, Palmer and I, or so I thought. Then I started to receive some mysterious letters. The first was stuck under the wiper blade of my car – I found it one night as I was leaving work."

Waiting for Zoe to carry on, Tara urges her on when she doesn't. "So, what did it say?"

"Keep your hands off Palmer. He's mine!" Zoe recalls, word for word.

Brows raised, Tara snorts a laugh, "Short and to the point – did you find out who sent it?"

"No, and others soon followed," Zoe frowns remembering. "They were all short, like sharp daggers sent straight to the heart."

"And the others, they were along the same lines?"

Nodding, Zoe looks up from her works to look Tara in the eyes. "He had an excuse for everything, though he couldn't explain why the notes accused him of being a father to a child he didn't care about. He just said it was rubbish and that I shouldn't believe it."

"I'll bet he did!" Tara blows a noisy breath out as her eyes widen. "Do you think it was true?"

"I didn't...but now I don't know." Her voice has softened, her eyes misting over. "I hate to think that he could have fooled me so completely. The thought of him having another child out there, one he doesn't give a damn about, only makes me hesitate even more when it comes to letting him know that I'm pregnant."

Sitting up straighter, Tara huffs loudly. "If I were you I'd keep that bit of news to yourself. At least until you can find out for sure. I mean, you don't want him marching down here trying to stake some sort of claim in a bid to get you back into his life!"

Shaking her head, Zoe stops pretending to work on the arrangement and folds her hands in her lap.

"He doesn't know where I am – no one does," Zoe explains. "Well, except for my dad and he's the one who bought me the cottage."

Tara's eyes go wide and round again, "You mean, he actually bought it for you...lock stock and barrel – no mortgage?"

"I know, I couldn't believe it either," Zoe tells her. "He's only recently come back into my life after leaving me and my mum when I was a toddler. He fell for his leading lady!"

Now Tara is frowning. "Leading lady? Is he an actor then?"

Laughing at the complexity of her story, Zoe shakes her head at the wonder of it. "His name is Douglas Benson, he's very well known in Hollywood."

Spluttering, Tara's eyes are now large as saucers. "Not just in Hollywood – I've got all of his films. I absolutely love your dad! He's gorgeous and so...so..." Lost for words, Tara just flays her hands expressively.

"I know," Zoe laughs at her new friend. "He really is something to look at. I feel quite shabby when I'm anywhere near him."

"Don't be ridiculous!" Tara rebukes. "You've got quite the look of him, now that I know to look for it."

"Do you really think so?" Zoe grins delighted. "I've only ever compared myself to my mother, but I'd like to think I have something of my father about me too."

Nodding rapidly, Tara is eager for more news. "Tell me

all the gossip – has he got anyone new in his life romantically speaking? Oh I hope not, it's kind of nice imagining that it could be me!"

"Tara! You're a married woman with two lovely children," Zoe rebukes, startled by her boss's revelation.

"And don't I know it!" Tara replies. With a loud tut she asks, "Don't you have any fantasies? Little dreams that help relieve the boredom of everyday life?"

Nonplussed, Zoe shakes her head. "I've never thought about it. But you wouldn't really be unfaithful to your husband...would you?"

Her boss's face goes soft and a smile tugs at her lips. "Not on your life! I love my old man, and the kids are an added bonus – a God-given joy that I give thanks for every single day. But it doesn't hurt to imagine myself as a sexy, attractive woman that someone like Douglas Benson might actually take a passing interest in!"

"Well, I'm glad to hear it. And I'm sure he'd have more than a passing interest in you if you weren't already taken," Zoe tells her honestly. "You have a terrific figure even though you've had two children – I hope I'm as lucky after my baby is born."

Tara shakes her head. "Unless you're one of those hateful women who can get back into their jeans the day after the birth, you'll have to do what the rest of us do.

Pop the baby out and then pump up the volume on a good exercise DVD. I had to lose 18lbs after I had my last one!"

Zoe's eyes goggle as she regards Tara. "I would never have thought that! You look so slim and toned – how did you manage to lose it all?"

"Breast feeding is great for a starting point – it takes a hell of a lot of calories to keep a baby happily fed on breast milk alone," Tara tells her. "And then it's down to hard work and determination. I hated being fat, so I got stuck into diet and exercise right off the bat!"

"Yes, well, you have a man to please – I don't know that I'll have the motivation to make the effort," Zoe admits.

"But you already take care of yourself," Tara observes with a nod of approval. "Unless you *are* one of those hateful women who can eat all they want and still stay slim. I'm really gonna hate you if you tell me you are!"

"I don't have a choice in the matter at the moment," Zoe reminds her. "I'm lucky if my food stays down long enough to be digested!"

"Hmm, and that's not good – have you been to the doctor?"

Hanging her head, Zoe shakes it forlornly. "I really don't like the idea of taking medication while I'm pregnant. And all the books say that morning sickness usually calms down after the first 8 to 12 weeks. I think I'll hang on and see what happens."

"Ok. I can understand that, but don't be a martyr to it. If it gets too bad there are things they can give you that won't harm the baby," Tara advises, concerned for Zoe's already slim stature.

"Oh my god..." Tara suddenly screams excitedly, "...I have Douglas Benson's real life daughter working for me. Aaaahhhh!!!!"

They both giggle like school-girls at Tara's excitement, then calm into a more serious mood.

"I miss my life," Zoe admits when her laughter dies down. "Don't get me wrong, I couldn't wish for a better second home, but I miss my mother, and stupidly, I still miss Palmer."

"So, the notes, are they what made you leave Palmer?" Tara asks solemnly.

"Yes. The final one arrived on our wedding day attached to a lovely bouquet of flowers," Zoe smiles ruefully. "Just like the ones we send out every day."

"On your wedding day! You mean you left him at the altar?"

"I did, yes." And Zoe's eyes mist over at the memory of that awful day. "I went into the bedroom to get some alone time – the place was a hive of activity and I just needed to get away from it all for a while."

Falling silent, Zoe can still see it in her mind's eye as if it were yesterday.

"My maid-of-honour had taken delivery of the flowers earlier and I'd asked her to put them in my bedroom for me." Her brows draw together as she remembers turning the note that came with the flowers over in her hand. "The attached envelope was larger than usual; I remember thinking that was odd at the time. But it wasn't overly large, and I just thought that Palmer had probably asked them to deliver a personal note with the flowers." Looking up at Tara, Zoe says, "We do that, right. We send personal messages with flowers all the time."

"Yes," Tara agrees. "It was a perfectly reasonable assumption."

"Only...it wasn't from Palmer. It was one of 'those' notes, only this one had a couple of small photos attached as a bonus." Rubbing her hands over her face, Zoe tries to obliterate the hurtful memory. "It was Palmer...he was kissing someone who definitely wasn't me. He lied to me. He lied all along."

"Hell!" Tara reaches out to take Zoe's now trembling hands. "Forget the bastard! And give God thanks that you didn't find the note after you were married to the shitbag!"

Zoe laughs then bursts into tears. "I'm so stupid! I honestly believed him! I'm such an idiot!"

"No, sweetie," Tara jumps up to put an arm around her young employee's shoulders. "Men can be such bastards! Don't you go blaming yourself, just because he could lie so well, damn it!"

"I'm sorry, blubbering all over you," Zoe says, having taken the ball of tissues Tara has thrust into her hands. "I seem to cry at the drop of a hat these days. And the worst of it is, I still love the jerk!"

CHAPTER FOUR

In his hotel suite, Connor relaxes back on one of the large settees to read the report a PI has just given to him.

"And you're sure it's her – you're absolutely positive?" he demands.

The PI he's hired to find Zoe stands in the middle of the room watching Connor nod and smile at his report's contents.

"If you take a look in that envelope I gave you, you'll be able to judge for yourself," the PI's gravelly voice points out.

Picking up the A5 envelope that he had discarded, Connor takes out a handful of photos that show Zoe at work, walking on the street, and going into a quaint cottage that he assumes is her new home.

Holding that particular photo up for the PI's inspection, Connor asks him, "Is this where she lives?"

"Yes, sir, it is. As well as the week of day time observations, I did a 24 hour surveillance, just as you asked. She came home from working at the florists and didn't leave again until work the next morning," he reports brusquely. "She had no visitors in all the time I was observing her."

"So no male interest that you could determine," Connor asks, wanting to be sure.

"No, sir, not that I saw."

"Good. Good. What's your name?" Connor asks as he peruses the man's report again.

"Its Grady, sir. Tom Grady, but I prefer Grady," the PI insists quietly.

"Well, Grady, I'm delighted with your work. Here..." Connor gets up; pulling out his wallet he gives the PI a delighted smile, "...a bonus for a job well done. I have a feeling I could use your services in the near future – can I count on you?"

"Yes, sir!" Grady doesn't even bother to count the notes Connor has given him. Their £50 denomination is enough to tell him that he's just been given a handsome tip. "You have my personal number, just call when you need me."

"Does that mean that I won't have to go through the agency?" Connor clarifies.

"If that's how you'd like to deal with things, that's fine by me," Grady acknowledges.

Nodding, Connor regards the man and judges him to be trustworthy. "I have a few dealings that are not exactly illegal but are, shall we say, not what I would want to have bandied about. Are you game to assist me with this?"

Grady doesn't hesitate. He's been paid well and if the man asks him to do something blatantly illegal he can always refuse at the time. But for now, "Yes sir. Day or night, just call me on the private number I gave you and if I'm free I'll get right to you."

"If you're free?"

"I work for the agency primarily," the PI speaks plainly. "I would have to carry out any jobs that I'm booked for. But in between time, I would be all yours, sir."

"How much do you earn a year, Grady?" Connor asks bluntly, watching the man for signs of lying.

"I make around £25K a year, plus expenses," the PI tells him quickly and honestly.

"If I offered you £30K a year plus expenses, would you take it?"

Again, the PI doesn't hesitate — he can sense a new

and lucrative career opportunity and decides to take a chance. "Yes sir, I would."

"You're hired! You work for me from now on and your first job is to deliver an envelope and pick up a payment," Connor tells him, again watching the man for signs of anything untoward.

"When and where?" Grady asks.

"I'll let you know as soon as I do. Then I want you back on Zoe Benson's tail," Connor orders, his blood surging with his newfound power.

I may not be a millionaire yet but I am well on my way. And in the meantime, the big man will be toppled from his high and mighty throne! He's already grumbling about losing a few contracts that he'd expected to bag.

Watch this space, bro, I'm comin' to get ya'.

Craig Stanley watches a delivery of concrete being poured into the footings of the new Community Centre they've begun to build, then turns his eyes to watch Palmer stride his way across the site to his side.

"How's it going?" Palmer asks as he comes alongside Craig.

"No problems so far," Craig's rich brown voice observes. "Have you heard anything from Connor? Has he turned up at home yet?"

Frowning with annoyance, Palmer rubs his tired eyes

then looks all the way up to meet the big guy's concerned gaze.

"He phoned our mother a couple of weeks ago, but nothing since," Palmer tells him. "Christ knows what he's living on, he hasn't picked up any wages from me since he downed tools and left."

"Hmm, weird!" Craig nods his head in consideration. "Not like he has that many options – I mean, he isn't skilled in any other area that I know of. Not that he was all that skilled in the building trade either!"

"Yes, I know. But he is my brother, if he comes on site just put him to work and let me know," Palmer tells him, though he knows he's being more optimistic than realistic.

"Will do, boss."

"How is Carly taking all this business with Zoe doing a disappearing act? Has she heard from her yet?"

Craig shifts uncomfortably and he becomes fascinated by the pattern his boots are etching in the dust.

"She has!" Palmer guesses before the big man can answer him. "Is she alright? Where is she? Craig! Where the hell is she?" Palmer demands when his friend doesn't answer.

Frowning deeply, Craig lifts his eyes to look at his boss and friend. "I don't know where she is," he tells him, then quickly holds up a stilling hand when Palmer makes to jump in. "I don't, and that's the truth. Zoe writes to her mother but she mails them to her dad in America first and he posts them on to Carly." Scratching his head, Craig grimaces, "She told her mother not to tell you anything in case you worked out somehow where she's living. She doesn't want to see you," he adds quietly. "Said she got a couple of photos in with the letter that came with the flowers – they apparently show you kissing some other woman."

Palmer's eyes go round as saucers and the breath is knocked clean out of his lungs.

Bending over with his hands on his knees, Palmer has to steady himself or keel over in the dirt. *They don't exist. There can't be a photo of me kissing anyone other than Zoe – I never have!*

"Damn it, Craig, I never cheated on Zoe!" he tells his friend hotly. "So whatever she says she's got, it's a lie. I never cheated on her, I love her, damn it!"

Craig never believed that Palmer would cheat on Zoe, he just isn't that kind of a man. But if he didn't, how come Zoe says she's got photos that show him doing just that? He doesn't believe that Zoe would lie either.

"I don't know what's going on, but Carly is sure that Zoe wouldn't lie either. And I'm inclined to believe her, too."

Palmer gapes at his friend, feeling like he's just been punched in the gut.

"You think I cheated on her?"

"I didn't say that," Craig shakes his head firmly. "I said I don't know what's going on. But I don't believe Zoe would have deliberately lied. Her mother told me about their last few months together, working on the wedding and enjoying some real mother and daughter time." Craig toes the dust again, his eyes following the movements. "Carly told me that even on the wedding day, Zoe looked excited to be getting married – it was only when she got that letter that things changed."

"You mean when she got the photos," Palmer corrects angrily. "Damn it, Craig – you know me! You know I wouldn't cheat on Zoe. You have to convince Carly to let me read those letters. I need to find Zoe and get a look at those photos!"

The frown between his brows grows deep with concern. "Not sure I can do that," he tells Palmer. "Carly is only just getting herself back together. She was devastated when Zoe just up and left."

"You...you believe her," Palmer gapes at Craig with his heart torn open by the unjust accusation in his friend's averted eyes.

"I'm not saying I believe you cheated on Zoe," Craig

lifts his eyes to look at Palmer directly. "But I am saying that you need to think hard about what you did do! Did you meet an old girlfriend and give her a hello kiss that someone managed to get on film, something like that?"

Palmer actually stops pacing and tries to think. Yes, that could be it - but he can't remember anything like that happening.

Heaving out a loud sigh, Palmer shakes his head. "That was a good thought, but no, I don't remember anything like that happening. Now what?" he asks, pushing both hands back through his blond hair.

"I don't know," Craig sighs just as heavily. "I'll keep my ears open and let you know what I can."

Palmer's world is falling apart. First he lost Zoe, and now his business is in trouble. It was coasting along nicely a few short weeks ago but now it's struggling - he hasn't won a single significant contract in the last couple of months. If things carry on in this vein he's going to be forced into decisions that he'd rather not contemplate until he absolutely has to.

Dorothy Johnson is a mother with the world on her shoulders. Both her sons appear to be in trouble and she can't fathom a way to help either of them.

I've never seen Palmer so distracted – even given that he's been devastated by Zoe leaving him, there seems to be more going on than meets the eye.

And what the heck is going on with Connor? He didn't even take any of his belongings with him.

How can he suddenly afford to throw in his job with Palmer then move out without taking a stitch with him? Which, of course, means that he's had to pay out for everything new again!

Sitting in her conservatory, Dorothy looks out over the beautiful garden that she takes such pride in. She would give anything to have her family back together, whole and thriving as it once had been.

Why is it always Connor that pains my heart so? Even as a boy he couldn't seem to get along with his brother, or even his other playmates. He's one on his own, and no mistake.

If only he could have learned from Palmer, he's always been such a good example for Connor. He mixed well with others as he was growing up, whereas Connor seemed to prefer his own company.

Why was that? He just didn't seem to know how to share — either his toys or his time. He hated doing what anyone else suggested, and he hasn't changed.

Oh, Connor, Connor...I just don't know what I did wrong, or what I can do now to make things better. And a mother should know. I should know!

At work the following day, Palmer calls Laura into his office and tries to get to the bottom of what is going on with his brother.

"Take a seat," he tells her, more abruptly than he realises.

Quaking inside, Laura just hopes this isn't about her lending Connor her works keys. He gave them back the next day so she doesn't see what the harm could be.

"Are you still seeing my brother," Palmer asks bluntly. "On a personal level, I mean."

Laura isn't slow, her hesitation in answering him is purely because she doesn't know the answer herself.

"I haven't seen Connor for a few weeks now," she admits, her head bowed and her eyes filled with sadness. "So I'm afraid I can't answer that properly, I can only guess that he's moved on. He never actually said anything...just stopped calling and coming round," she tells him, her voice suddenly trembling and her eyes filling with tears.

She has tried so very hard to get over Connor. To not let him matter. But every time her phone rings her heart leaps and fills with hope, only to be let down again and again.

Palmer watches Laura struggle to hold the tears back, and when he's sure that she is failing, passes her a box of tissues that he's learned to keep handy.

"I'm sorry, Laura. Sorry that you ever got involved with him," Palmer frowns, his already broken heart aching at the pain he knows she is suffering. "He doesn't deserve you."

"But I love him," she declares hopelessly. "And I know you'll think I'm stupid, but I'd welcome him with open arms if he'd just pick up the damned phone!"

Giving a wry smile and a scathing low laugh, Palmer eyes his employee and wonders how it is that Connor, who obviously doesn't give a damn for this young woman, can have her eating out of his hand and begging to take even more of his crap!

I just can't fathom it! I loved Zoe with everything that I am – no, I love Zoe still with everything that I am. Yet I'm alone with no apparent way of getting her back. Where is the justice in that!

"So, you have no idea where he is?"

"No. We did spend the night in a Holiday Inn a few weeks back, but I've barely heard from him since."

"A Holiday Inn?" he asks, aghast at his brother's sudden affluence. "And where did he get the money for that?"

"I have no idea, but he seemed to have plenty," Laura said, remembering how Connor had thrown a handful of bank notes into the air from a bag that had looked full of them. But she decides not to tell Palmer about that.

"You do know that he's quit his job," he tells her, watching for any giveaway signs.

Nodding, Laura looks up at Palmer, "Macy in wages told me that she isn't making up his wages anymore. I think she was fishing for info," Laura explains when Palmer frowns over at her.

"And did you give her any," he asks.

"Nothing to give. I have no idea what is going on with Connor. I can only hope he does!"

CHAPTER FIVE

If there is one thing about Cornwall that you can rely on, no matter what the weather, it is the breath-taking views.

The day has started off overcast, but Zoe is still enjoying pottering about her garden and looking out over the Looe River. It looks slate grey today, but what little sunshine manages to seep through the clouds seems to shimmer over it like diamonds.

She's up especially early today, and plans to watch the fishermen auction off their catches on the quay and pick up some super fresh fish for herself. Tara has shown her how to cook and eat a freshly caught crab, and she plans to buy one if there are any to have.

Zoe has settled in to the fishing village life style well.

She loves the friendly locals, the way everyone waves now that they know she isn't just a tourist.

"Now then maid, you wanting a boilin' of muscles?" one fisherman asks as she walks along the edge of the key to see what is for sale.

"Not today, Ben," Zoe grins, loving the broad accent and olde worlde speak of the born and bred Cornishmen. "I'm after a good sized crab if I can find one?"

"See Tony, 'es got a couple oh good uns," Ben grins, the gaps in his teeth only making his accent even more difficult to understand.

Giving Ben a wave, Zoe goes in search of Tony. The two men have taken her under their wing, so to speak. Advising her on what's good in the catch and how to best go about cooking it.

And a good job too. Zoe's mother had done most of the cooking when she'd lived at home. Moving out on her own has been a real eye-opener.

"Mornin'," Tony tips an imaginary hat in Zoe's direction and grins a welcome. "Got somethin' I think yu'll like o'er 'ere," he tells her, walking over to a box with half a dozen live crabs in it. "Don't get no fresher 'en that, maid!"

Maid - her mother would have a fit of the giggles if she heard the way men referred to the women in

Cornwall. But she had no complaints, everyone was so friendly and the men only looking out for her.

It seems to have become common knowledge that she is expecting a 'babe'. And she'd heard a couple of the older men talking in Kernewek, the old Cornish language, and had caught the word *gour,* and what looked like a very curious look.

Later, she'd asked Tara about the word and had been shocked to realise that they were probably speculating on her lack of a 'husband', which is what gour means in Kernewek, or Cornish.

If she wore fitted clothes, Zoe was starting to 'show'. And Tara was encouraging when it came to Zoe being open about her pregnancy.

"You're here for the foreseeable future," she'd told her. "You're not going to be able to hide it for much longer so it makes sense to be open about it. Some people may lift their judgemental brows, but not many. Most will be supportive – you'll see!"

"They...look..."

"Alive," Tony's son, Jason, states with a mischievous grin.

"Yes," Zoe agrees with a laugh. "They certainly do look very much alive."

"Tis the best way, my ansum," Tony tells her with pride.

"But you don't fancy boiling them to death," Jason guesses, and laughs when he sees her blanch at the very idea. "Then choose the one you want and I'll bring it round to you later today," he offers, and Zoe tips her head to look at him curiously.

"You bought the old Trelawney cottage, didn't you," Jason states rather than asks. And when he sees her nod, he smiles, "Then I'll have it to you by 4 o'clock. That'll give you plenty of time to ready it for your tea."

Holding out her hand to him, Zoe smiles her thanks. "My name is Zoe, and I am very pleased to meet you."

Taking her hand, Jason reciprocates her greeting. "My name is Jason, and I think you're only very pleased to meet me because I'm going to boil that crab for you," he tells her, and they both enjoy a good laugh.

"That might have something to do with it," Zoe admits shyly. "But really, I'm happy to meet all of the locals. I couldn't have wished for kinder people to live amongst."

"And they don't take to foreigners easily," Jason tells her. "You must have some Celtic blood in your bones that eased your way into our hearts."

"You don't have the same accent that the men around here have," Zoe enquires with a curious frown.

Hoofing a thumb over his shoulder at Tony, Jason tells her, "My father was born and bred in Looe and never left it, ever," he states with a shake of his head. "I went to university in the Midlands, and was away for the best part of four years. My accent sort of thinned out through necessity – no one knew what the bloody hell I was talking about when I first arrived."

Laughing again, they walk to the end of the quay where Zoe gives him her thanks again.

"I'm really looking forward to having fresh crab for my tea," she smiles brightly. "I'll just have to pretend that I didn't see him walking around first, otherwise I don't think I could eat him."

Chuckling deeply, Jason lifts a hand to bid her good-morning, then makes his way back to his father.

Taking a slow walk to the beach, Zoe doesn't realise that she is being followed.

What a glorious sight! Only a few early birds, like me, about. Other than that, the beach is thankfully empty.

Taking her sandals off, Zoe steps onto the warm sand and scrunches her toes into it as she makes her way to the shoreline.

Even as she broaches it, Zoe can feel a stiff breeze blowing her way and pulls her cardigan tighter about her shoulders.

With an unconscious hand to her round belly, Zoe contemplates her future.

Would this be a good place to raise a child? The people are certainly friendly enough, and what child wouldn't love to have a beach as their playground! But I'd have to watch them like a hawk, and not just from the dangers of being drowned. Tourists come from every walk of life, who knows what kind of person could be sitting next to us on the beach while my son or daughter enjoys building sand-castles!

The thought gives Zoe the chills, and she walks back to the road and makes her way home.

Connor moves out of the shadows to stand watching the cottage. Grady had been right, Zoe was settled into her new life and didn't look like she would be coming back to Birmingham any time soon.

Now, how do I just happen to be here in Looe? I need a damned good excuse to bump into her. I'll need to give that some thought, but soon. I don't like the look of that fisherman. I doubt Zoe would look at a local yokel twice, but you never know. I need to get in quick!

Walking back to his car, Connor drives back to Millendreath where he is renting a luxury home that some rich bod was renting out for the summer while he was apparently off working somewhere in America.

I could bring Zoe here. She'd love to swim in the private pool, and wouldn't she be impressed!

Spotting Grady on his laptop in the lounge, Connor moves over to the man to see what he's up to.

"You gamble on line?" Connor scoffs loudly. "Isn't that like standing on a cliff and throwing you money into the wind? Though I'm sure it would be more entertaining to watch it flutter away in front of you than just disappearing it out of your bank account with the press of a button!"

Grady looks up with a sullen scowl. "I only make small bets and it's just for a bit of fun. I tend to break even as long as I don't up the ante to try and win my losses back."

"I have a job for you," Connor tells him as he crosses to a small bar and pours himself a shot of whiskey. "There's a young guy on the quay in Looe, obviously a fisherman...or some such shit...I want to know everything there is to know about him, and quick."

Grady closes the lid on his laptop and stands ready to do Connor's bidding. "Got a name and description for me?"

"Yes, I heard him introduce himself to Zoe as Jason...no last name given," Connor adds. "He's about my height and age, his hair is dark and almost shoulder length, and he was wearing a red and black t-shirt with some band name or other scrawled on the back of it. I didn't see anyone else dressed like him so you shouldn't have any difficulty picking him out. But you'd better leave now to be on the safe side."

Grady moves to the door then turns when his boss calls his name.

"Grady, the man he was talking to was named Tony – I think that's his dad."

Grady gives Connor a nod then continues on his way to find and track the man.

Looking out over the sea view, Connor sips his whiskey then opens the large sliding doors and steps out onto a large patio. With his whiskey in hand he walks around the edge of a huge pool then strips of his clothes to go skinny dipping.

His lean body has taken well to the Cornish sunshine. His muscles gleam golden as he tears through the water.

He's always been a good swimmer, and finds it a relaxing and enjoyable way to stay fit - though the house came with a well equipped gym that he has also made good use of.

Turning onto his back, Connor floats lazily in the early morning sun.

By mid-morning no doubt it will be roasting. But right now...aahhh, this is great!

You can stick your loft living bro', I'm getting me a place just like this soon as I can!

Grady walks onto the quay and catches the last of the

fishermen just packing away. He hasn't spotted the man he's after but...

"Yes!" he grunts quietly to himself, as none other than Jason stands up from sorting out his father's trays.

Moving away, Grady takes up a covert position from which to watch his quarry and make a few notes. The van's registration plate on to which he is loading the empty trays, and the registration of a nearby car Grady has observed him go to.

It's a long day for Grady; he follows Jason when he goes home and later when he delivers the cooked crab to Zoe, and in between time it's all about watching and waiting. Something Grady is good at.

Knocking on her door, Jason waits for Zoe to answer and can't work out why he's so nervous.

"Jason..." Zoe smiles a warm welcome, "...you're earlier than I'd expected. Is that it?" she asks, pointing at the bag hanging at his side.

"It is, and I did the cooking of it myself," he adds proudly. "Though I have to admit the wine was my mother's idea, she said a small glass won't do you, or the baby, any harm."

"That's...nice..." Zoe hesitates, her smile faltering.

"I'm sorry...did I say something wrong?" he asks innocently, holding the bottle of white wine out to her.

"It's just...I'm not sure...I mean..." Shaking her head to dismiss her unease, Zoe props her smile back in place and invites Jason in. "I've made a salad up with cold potatoes and chopped raw mushrooms if you'd care to join me. After all, you did cook the crab."

Straightening his back with pride, Jason returns her smile and nods, "I did didn't I. That would be very nice, if you're sure?"

Grady waits for three hours; finally, Jason emerges from the cottage.

"That was the best crab tea I've ever had," Jason tells Zoe when he takes his leave. "But I'll deny I ever said so if it gets back to me mam!"

Having enjoyed his company, Zoe laughs promising not to tell a soul. She hasn't had so much fun in...well...not since Palmer, and is shocked by the thought.

Driving back to Millendreath, Grady gets his thoughts straight before he arrives back at his boss's temporary home.

He knows what Connor will expect; a blow by blow account of the day and an exact time for how long Jason spent with Zoe Benson.

"What the hell was he doing in there, screwing her!" Connor explodes when Grady gives him his report.

"I don't know sir. He brought something in a bag and a

bottle of white wine – he wasn't carrying anything when he left," Grady adds pointedly.

"So you said! Damn it!" Connor slams his hand down on the arm of his chair angrily. "I need to get in there before she takes up with someone else!"

Getting to his feet, Connor paces the lounge then looks at his mobile when it beeps to indicate a message received.

"I need you to pick up an envelope back in Birmingham," he tells Grady, shoving his phone back in his pocket. "Same as before, ok?"

"Yes sir. When would you want me to leave?"

"Morning will do. You'll have time to do a bit of surveillance. I want to know what's going on with Palmer and Laura," Connor demands. "Spend a couple of days checking them out then get back here."

Giving a nod of acknowledgement, Grady asks, "Do you need me for anything else tonight?" And when Connor shakes his head continues, "Then I'll be in my room, if that's alright?"

"Sure, just let me know if you go out," Connor tells him as he makes his way over to the bar to refill his whiskey.

I'll be seeing you soon, Zoe Benson. Then we'll see which brother you prefer!

CHAPTER SIX

Looking at himself in the mirror, Connor straightens his hair and puts a little gel on to keep the shaggy style in place.

That should do it! Keep it casual, let her think you're just here on holiday and it's all a big coincidence that you've run into her.

Now put your best foot forward and treat her like a lady. No...a queen to be treasured and looked after. And I will. You are going to be mine, Zoe Benson. All mine!

The drive to Looe is beautiful, but Connor barely notices. His mind is focused on one thing, Zoe! He knows she works 3 mornings a week at the florists; he's read and re-read Grady's report until he can remember her usual activities off-by-heart. Now he's going to put all that knowledge to good use.

It's almost 1 o'clock by the time he reaches Looe and parks his car. He'd managed to get a spot right on the river front, opposite the Estate Agents.

Walking casually, Connor goes into a little café and orders himself a cup of coffee then sits by the window and waits.

Sure enough, Zoe walks by the window at 1:15 and he bolts from his seat and into Fore Street.

"Hey, Zoe," he calls, and watches her turn in confusion. "It's me, Connor, what the hell are you doing down here?" he asks innocently.

"I...I could ask you the same thing," Zoe tells him, paling visibly and reaching a hand out to a shop wall to steady herself.

"I'm on holiday; you...?" he asks.

"I...I...please Connor, just forget you saw me," she tells him, turning on her heals and walking as fast as she can away from him.

But her luck isn't that good. Connor isn't going away and he isn't going to forget that he's seen her. *Now what?!*

"Hey, hey," Connor catches up and takes her arm, gently pulling Zoe to a stop. "I'm not my brother," he tells her softly, "I'm not going to hurt you."

She wants to laugh, this is Connor, the man who

blacked Laura's eye telling her that he won't hurt her like he's some sort of hero.

"I know who you are and what you're capable of," Zoe tells him, shrugging her arm out of his grasp. "So don't play the good-guy with me!"

She watches a shutter come down on his face, but sees a hint of sadness before he can hide it.

"Of course you do," Connor frowns at his feet. "But you were taken in by Palmer, just like everyone else. Why wouldn't you believe I'm a no good waster. I'll see you around, Zoe."

Stunned and confused, Zoe watches Connor walk away, his shoulders slumped and his head bowed.

Have I got this wrong? Do I know Connor, what he's really like?

"Wait!" Trotting up to him, Zoe takes his arm and draws alongside Connor. "Wait. Let's just talk. It can't hurt to talk, right?"

Hesitating, Connor pretends to be weighing up his options; in reality he's wondering what to do next so as not to overplay his hand. "Right. Do you want to go for a walk; I haven't had a chance to explore yet?"

"Ok," Zoe agrees, and they both smile partly in relief but for their own very different reasons.

"So, where are you staying," Connor asks, as they

continue to meander up Fore Street into the main town centre.

"I have a small cottage," Zoe tells him, unsure about how much to tell him. "My father helped me after...after..."

"It's alright, you don't have to talk about back then – I just wanted to know you're alright now?" Connor reassures her quietly.

"Yes, yes I am, really." Zoe smiles brightly and begins to realise that she is alright, she isn't just spouting the words.

"That's good. I'm pleased for you. Are you working at all?"

"Yes, but you'd never guess what I'm doing," she giggles girlishly.

Oh I wouldn't bet on that!

"Is it something really bizarre like pole dancing," Connor laughs, and when Zoe has gotten over the shock of his suggestion, she laughs too.

"No, it is not pole dancing! As if I could ever do that kind of thing?"

"Well it wouldn't be out of your realm of possibilities," Connor continues to laugh, enjoying her embarrassment. "You're a beautiful woman, men would definitely pay to see you pole dance!"

"Connor, Please!" Zoe looks left and right, hoping that no one has overheard their outlandish conversation. "I live here now, I don't want people hearing you suggest that I...do...that!" she tells him, her hands waving expressively in front of her.

"Alright, no more career suggestions," he chuckles softly. "So what do you do?"

Her pale cheeks redden as she tells him, "I work in a florist shop. I sell flowers and I help to make up the arrangements."

Lifting a brow, Connor stares at her, "Don't you need some kind of training to do that? I thought you went to college to be a PA, like you were for Palmer?"

"I did, and if you want to make a career out of floristry you probably do need proper training," Zoe acknowledges. "But Tara is happy with what I do, she just gives me an idea of what she wants and a little guidance along the way."

"Sounds like you're a natural."

Laughing, enjoying the sun and the sea breeze as they come upon the beach, Zoe feels lighter than she has in months. "Thankfully, that's what Tara thinks too, or I'd be out of a job."

"It sounds nice," Connor frowns out to sea, "the life you have here."

And your life, Connor, isn't your life nice?

"You sound sad," Zoe observes quietly as they stare out over Looe Bay and the English Channel.

The wind catches Connor's dark hair and blows it across his eyes. Behind the pretext of brushing it away, Connor takes the chance to study Zoe, to see what she's thinking.

"Not sad, just..." He lets the thought hang in the air, his brows drawn together over brooding eyes. "I've moved on too," he tells her. "I don't work for Palmer anymore and I haven't seen Laura in a lot of weeks."

"You broke up!"

"Why so shocked, you didn't like me seeing her anyway," he tells her bluntly.

"It was just...well...look Connor, you deliberately bated me," she tells him hotly. "What you did was indecent."

He doesn't pretend not to understand, but his lazy smile gives him an attractive bad boy look. "It was wasn't it? But you were so naive, and so...so...damn it; I wanted it to be you!"

That shocks her into stunned silence, and her eyes go wide at the thought.

"What, don't tell me you didn't think of that?" he asks. Then realises that she hadn't. "I wanted you so bad that I almost took you forcefully in that car park — only that's not the way I wanted it to be between us. But you only had eyes for 'the big man' and he wasn't even being faithful to you! What a joke!"

Shaking her head, Zoe backs away. "No, Connor. It wouldn't have been right then and it certainly wouldn't be right now."

"Still too wrapped up in Palmer, even though he's been outed," Connor looks disgusted and begins to walk away.

But Zoe is hurting and Connor has made her feel like an idiot. "How was I to know? He told me he loved me," she shouts when he keeps on walking.

He turns then, tipping his head to one side to regard her. "Is that all it takes Zoe — just whisper sweet nothings in your ears and you'll keep falling at his feet?"

When he turns to keep walking, Zoe rushes forward to catch his arm and turn him around angrily. "You think you know me, but you don't! I loved him! It wasn't just a romantic fling, I still love him...and it hurts, what he did to me. It really hurts!"

Once her tears break free she can't stop them, and Zoe finds herself being held by the last man she'd ever have imagined.

"It alright," he croons softly, rocking her as she gulps

for air between body-wrenching sobs. "I'm here, at least you can cry on my shoulder, if nothing else!"

And she does. Zoe lets go of months of tears that she's kept bottled up, and isn't the least bit concerned that she is in a public place. It just feels so good to finally let go, and to be held again, even if it is by Connor.

Pulling a handkerchief out of his pocket, Connor offers it to her and Zoe eventually pulls herself together. "Thanks, I needed that," she smiles ruefully. "The tears and the hanky."

"It sounds like they were a long time coming," Connor observes quietly, and Zoe nods in agreement. "Well, I'll be around for the next couple of weeks if you need a shoulder," he smiles, his blue eyes even bluer in the sun. And taking out a business card, he gives her his mobile telephone number.

"Call me, night or day, if you need that shoulder," he tells her as they walk towards a sea front bench.

"Where are you staying?" she asks curiously.

"You wouldn't believe it," he grins. "I don't believe it," he laughs. "It's a five bed house with its own swimming pool and a terrific sea view in Millendreath."

"Connor! Did you win the lottery, or what?"

Still laughing he says, "Nope. Just went out on my own and the business has taken off."

"What business — you don't work for Palmer anymore?"

"Not a chance. I finally found the guts to break free of them all," he tells her. "I got so sick of always being compared to Palmer. Why can't you be more like your brother, or look at how well Palmer is doing why don't you take a leaf out of his book." Shaking his head, Connor looks so sad, and more than a little angry.

"When you're a kid you kind of expect it; parents often use older siblings as a prime example of good behaviour. But..." He can't go on, the hurt goes deeper than even he imagined and his heart is still sore and bleeding.

Looking out to sea, Connor eventually gets himself together.

Turning to smile at Zoe, he catches an unshielded look of real concern that knocks the wind out of him.

Putting a hand on his arm, Zoe feels her tears gathering again, only this time they are for Connor, and it tears at her.

"I'm so sorry, Connor, I'm as guilty as all the rest..." she tells him sadly "...I didn't look beyond the surface."

"No probs'" he shrugs, but he likes that she cares.

"Would you like to see it?" he asks suddenly, shaking Zoe out of her doldrums.

"See what?" she asks, not having followed his train of thought.

"The house where I'm staying," he smiles and rolls his eyes. "It's worth a look, I'm telling you."

"Well...I..."

His face clouds over and he turns to look back out to sea. "That's ok. I'd better be getting off, can I at least give you a lift somewhere?"

Hesitating, Zoe sucks in her bottom lip and chews on it for a second, then, "I'd love to. See the house," she adds when his brows furrow.

"You would?" And his grin is so boyish Zoe can't resist, her own grin as bright as his.

"Yes, I would."

During the walk back to his car, Connor feels like his feet are hovering six inches off the ground. He hadn't expected to feel this way; Zoe was supposed to be a tool to use against Palmer. But she is turning into something more, something unexpected and pleasant.

The drive isn't long; Millendreath is only a short way up the coast from Looe. But it is comfortable and beautiful, and the two enjoy each other's easy company.

For Zoe, Connor is an unexpected connection to her past; one she is realising it is harder to leave behind than she'd originally thought.

When she'd asked her father to help her move as far away as possible, she had thought severing the ties completely was the only way. Only, she hadn't realised how painful her decision would be to live by, or how lonely it would make her.

Now, here is Connor, making pleasant small talk and taking her to his holiday home in his fancy car.

Before long, they approach a set of wrought iron gates and Connor presses the remote to open them.

Zoe gapes at the opulence of her surroundings. "You're staying here? This must be costing you a small fortune to rent!"

Getting out of the car, Connor rounds the bonnet and takes her arm to escort her indoors.

"You ain't seen nothin' yet," he tells her, jiggling his eyebrows comically and making her laugh.

They walk through the large main doors into an atrium with large tropical looking plants, then into a sunken lounge with extra large settees framing the centre space.

"Connor..." Zoe breaths, her eyes flitting everywhere trying to take in her magnificent surroundings. "This is...amazing."

He laughs, pleased by her reaction. "Yes, it is isn't it. Come on, let's go out to the pool." And taking her hand he leads her outdoors.

No words come out of Zoe's mouth as it drops open, her rounded eyes taking in the amazing panoramic view of the English Channel and the surrounding countryside.

Shaking her head in stunned disbelief, Zoe walks round the pool and looks back at the house. "Wow, Connor. I mean...wow!" she says again, completely lost for words.

"You can take a dip, if you want to," he offers, his grin wide and excited by her reaction. But when he sees her blush he rushes on, "There are bathing suits and everything," he assures her. And then his mischievous side takes over, "You thought I was asking you to go skinny dipping, didn't you?" And when her blush deepens he says, "Well, it's an option, no one will see you from here."

No one but you. How did I get myself into this? Pregnancy must be addling my brains!

"Not for me it isn't," she tells him firmly. But adds a smile when Connor's starts to fade. "But thanks for the offer."

With his boyish grin back in place, Connor tells her, "There really are swimsuits if you'd like to take a dip. It might be nice to cool off a bit."

That water really does look inviting, and it's not like anyone else would know.

"Ok. Let's see what there is."

Stunned by her unexpected acceptance, Connor is at first rooted to the spot, then leaps forward to show her the way to his bedroom and the wardrobe that has various swimwear hanging in it.

Leaving her to change, Connor goes back to the pool and lies down on one of the sun-loungers having stripped down to his boxers.

When she reappears on the patio a few minutes later, he can't tear his eyes away from Zoe. Then she realises why.

"Oh god, Connor, I didn't think. Please, you can't tell anyone; especially not Palmer!"

He is staring straight at her swollen stomach and his eyes are disbelieving.

Pregnant! Zoe is pregnant!

"How far along are you?" he asks in a stupefied daze.

"Not long, it must have happened just before the wedding; I didn't even know myself," she tells him, a protective hand laid over her belly.

"So it is Palmers," he states bitterly. He doesn't even know why he's angry, but he really doesn't like the idea of his brother's baby being inside Zoe. "Damn the man!"

"I should go," Zoe turns, her eyes burning with humiliation and tears.

But Connor won't hear of it. Leaping from his lounger, he takes Zoe's arm and turns her gently. "It doesn't matter, and he won't hear about it from me."

Her bottom lip trembles badly, she's been so lonely, so cut off from everything and everyone.

Looking into her sad brown eyes, Connor feels himself falling into her. "It's ok. We'll make it ok." Then his lips close in on hers and take them gently, lovingly.

I should stop this. It isn't right. But he feels so good. So solid. So real.

Only when she feels his hand cover her breast does Zoe call a halt. "I'm sorry, Connor, I can't do this." And she reluctantly pulls out of his arms.

His diamond blue eyes are afire with a passion that surprises him. Taking a step away from her, Connor drags in a breath to steady himself.

"Take a swim, I'm going indoors to make a few calls," he tells her, then marches away leaving her all alone.

<u>CHAPTER SEVEN</u>

Watching from the lounge, Conner sees Zoe dive into the pool and strike out in a front crawl. She looks heavenly, and he can't stop watching her.

His plans have been shot to hell. He'd wanted to use her, to throw her in his brother's face as yet another conquest. But now...

Pushing his hands back through his dark hair, Conner can't seem to think straight.

Now what? I have no idea how to make her look at me without thinking about Palmer. Damn it! Damn him!

Pacing the lounge he eventually moves to the bar and pours himself a double whiskey. Then he pours Zoe a diet coke out of the mini fridge.

Taking both drinks out to the poolside, Connor settles

himself back down on the lounger and watches Zoe wear herself out.

No doubt she's trying to blot the world out. But exhausting herself like that isn't going to do the trick. She has to face it sometime, and now is as good a time as any!

Moving to the pool, Connor calls her name and watches her head turn when she hears it, but Zoe strikes out even harder.

He stands, undecided for just a second, then dives in after her. They match each other stroke for stroke for a few laps, then he wraps his arm around her waist, bringing them both to a stop.

"You'll exhaust yourself," he tells her, "and that can't be good for the baby."

Then Zoe does something that surprises them both. She bursts into tears and wraps her arms about his neck, holding on for all she's worth.

Any other time, Connor would have taken advantage of the situation, but right now he can't bring himself to do so.

"It's ok. Don't cry," he pleads, holding her to him his hand stroking over her hair. "Please don't cry, Zoe."

But she can't stop, her world is a mess and the only person in it to offer comfort is the last man she would have thought to take it from.

Both their worlds are spinning on their axis in a direction opposite to where it should be.

Now what! Damn it man, you had a plan! You wanted to get back at Palmer, to make him really suffer, she wasn't meant to matter. She's nothing to you...

But Connor is having trouble believing his own thoughts and his resolve is slipping.

The following day is Zoe's day off and she spends it tending to her garden while mulling over thoughts of Connor.

He'd been so kind to her. She'd thrown herself into his arms and he hadn't even taken advantage.

Maybe that's down to the fact that I'm about four months pregnant! Not a turn on for most men. But what would I have done if he had kissed me again? I needed someone...and Connor was right there.

Heaving out a sigh, Zoe continues to pull up weeds and add a few more plants to her borders.

And what about Palmer – will Connor tell him? The old Connor would have loved to give his brother the bad news. But I sense a change in him. He isn't the brash Connor I thought I knew.

No wonder he gets so angry at people – if they're all like me and judge him on face value.

And what right did I have to judge him at all. I only

knew what others had told me, what if they were wrong? What if Connor isn't the bad boy everyone makes him out to be?

When Grady gets back with Connor's cash he fills him in on the info he wanted.

"The woman is doing all the usual things, like going to work, going home and doing a bit of shopping. Didn't see any love interest.

Palmer Johnson is another matter. He's struggling with something. He's on his mobile a lot, goes from site to site and spends long hours at the office afterwards. Again, no love interest that I saw."

"What makes you say he's struggling with something?" Connor asks curiously.

"Mannerisms, facial expressions," Grady explains. "It's all in here," and he hands Connor a typed up report.

"Ok. Now I want you to go back and do an in-depth report on Henry Snelson – I want everything that slug ever did or is doing," Connor sneers with hate in his eyes. "And after that I want everything you can find on one David Hickey – that man almost killed me. I'm going to pay him back with interest!"

Grady nods and makes a mental note not to piss off his new boss. *This man holds a grudge and then some!*

"Do you want me to leave right now?" Grady asks,

ready to do his boss's bidding at the drop of a hat.

"Yes, the sooner the better. I have plans for Hickey, and I want something on Snelson that I can use on him. So dig deep and stay in touch," he adds before Grady leaves.

Going out to the pool, Connor strips naked and stretches his arms up and out before diving headlong into the sparkling water.

His muscles ripple as he pulls himself at speed from one end of the pool to the other, time after time. When he's finished he stands like a god, water dripping off him like diamonds glinting in the mid-morning sun.

Now he's ready to see Zoe, and goes indoors to shower and change.

Arriving at her cottage, Connor holds the bunch of flowers he's bought her out in front of his face.

"Hello there," Zoe laughs, then is startled when Connor moves the flowers to reveal himself. "What a nice surprise, you didn't say you were calling in."

"Do I need an appointment?" he jokes on a half serious note.

"No, though you should know that I'm not always here," she tells him.

"I remember, you work three mornings a week at the florist shop," he recalls, and impresses her into the bargain.

"You were paying attention," she chuckles, moving to reach down a vase for the flowers.

"Here, let me get that," Connor jumps up and reaches down a tall black vase. "You shouldn't be stretching like that – not with the baby," he nods towards her rounded stomach.

Putting a hand over the bulge, Zoe looks up at Connor with a curious gleam in her eyes.

"Doesn't it bother you?" she asks. "I mean, when you kissed me yesterday...it didn't seem like it bothered you."

Bringing his hand down to touch her cheek, his fingers glide over her silky skin and move down her throat to the back of her neck.

A thrill runs down her spine and Zoe's breathing becomes short and shallow. *I want you. Oh my god, I really want you!*

When his lips meet hers, Zoe can't deny the pull she feels towards Connor. She may still love Palmer but he isn't here and he betrayed her. Connor is here and he isn't offering anything but comfort – no strings attached.

This time when Connors hand covers her breast, Zoe doesn't knock it away. She arches into him and his groan into her mouth leaves her instantly wet and wanting.

The flowers lay forgotten on the work top, and the embrace heats up with each passing second.

Wearing a short sun dress, Zoe is easily accessible to Connor's eager hands. He pushes into her panties and cups her heat, his expert fingers sliding over her clit back and forth then suddenly enter her with a demanding thrust.

Her knees almost buckle, her gasp of pleasure driving him on, and Connor lifts her onto the work top and moves between her parted knees.

When his mouth covers her, when his tongue slides beneath her panties and slicks over her clit, Zoe screams out with the pleasure coursing through her and holds his head in place.

"Connor!" Her body is trembling from the wash of an orgasm that makes every sinew of her being sing. "Please..." she begs, "...now."

He needs no further encouragement and stands to look deep into her blazing eyes. "I want you Zoe...I want all of you!"

Pulling his erection clear of his trousers, Connor slides Zoe to the edge of the work top and plunges into her as her legs move around his waist.

"Christ! Christ!" She almost topples him over the edge before he can get control, but Connor grits his teeth and steadies himself, then backs her up to the wall and plunges for all he's worth.

She holds on for dear life, her head falling back, her breathing erratic.

And Connor moves in on her exposed throat, kissing the jumping pulse and feeling the blood pound in her veins.

"Mine!" he shouts as his body builds to climax. "Mine!" he shouts again, and empties his seed into her as she shudders to climax around him.

Much later, as they lay on the settee in each other's arms, Zoe begins to feel guilty about her fling with Connor. *How did this happen? Am I so lonely that I would have done it with any willing male? Oh god, I hope not!*

Sensing the battle raging inside her, Connor strokes a hand down her hair as her head lays against his chest.

"Stop over thinking it!" he warns softly. "I care about you, I think I always have," he tells her, and watches Zoe lift her head to look quizzically at him. "I just didn't get a look in. If I had, that baby inside you might have been mine."

Zoe sits up abruptly, a cold fear sliding through her veins. "That isn't what this is about? You're not just interested in me because of Palmer?"

He knows what she is asking, and a couple of days ago she'd have been right on the money. "No, Zoe. I'm interested in you because you're a beautiful woman who attracted me right off the bat. I just wasn't quick enough to win you over."

"I'm not a prize," Zoe glares down at Connor, her guilt turning quickly to anger. "And I'm not something to be passed around between brothers!" And that thought, having been voiced, makes her gasp with pain and her eyes tear up.

"Damn it, Zoe. You're making this into something sordid, and it isn't!" Connor pulls himself more upright and reaches for her, but she evades him.

"It is. That's exactly what this is!" Her hands fly up to cover her face as she stands over him, looking down at the man who should by now be her brother-in-law. "Oh, Connor, what have we done!"

Moving to stand with her, Connor shoves his hands in his pockets knowing instinctively that Zoe won't let him hold her.

"I'm not going to apologise for wanting you," he tells her bluntly. "And you shouldn't feel guilty for wanting me. My brother doesn't deserve you. I'll take care of you. You and the baby," he adds, and watches her eyes widen in wonder.

"You...I don't understand...why would you? You have Laura, I'm sure she'd be more than happy to bear your children," she tells him, unable to fathom out Connor's motivation.

"I don't want Laura," he tells her, taking a step closer. "I never did – you already know that."

She does. Remembering the way he'd looked at her while kissing Laura, her stomach does a back-flip and her legs feel like jelly.

"I need to sit down," Zoe says, and moves to the settee with Connor sitting beside her. "You're telling me that you would look after me and my child...but what's in it for you? What could you possibly get out of such a one sided arrangement?"

He doesn't hesitate, doesn't take a moment to think it through. "You!"

One word, a single solitary syllable, but it conveys everything.

CHAPTER EIGHT

Palmer sorts through the tenders he's been putting in and lost. He needs to reassess them to find out why they were turned down.

Remembering a conversation he once had with Zoe's mother, Palmer now understands what she meant about being armed for survival.

If you want something more than the other person, you need to strategise and be determined. But even if you win, the loser also has to survive. And maybe one day the loser might be you!

Her words come back to him, sounding prophetic in the circumstances, and he ploughs on to do what she advised. To strategies!

His old friend, Craig Stanley, sits eating a well cooked meal at Carly's table.

"I'll say it again, Carly, you are a seriously good cook and I'm the luckiest man alive," he smiles before taking another mouthful of her home cooked steak and Kidney pie.

Blushing modestly, Carly is proud of her ability to please this giant of a man, and thinks back over their first night together.

It has taken a while for Carly to trust him, but Craig spent his first night in her bed last night. And what a night it had been for both of them.

Neither of them has been involved with anyone serious for a lot of years, and now they are moving cautiously on to the next stage in their relationship.

"I'm pleased you like it," she tells him, adding more gravy to his plate and receiving a smile of thanks. "I haven't had anyone but Zoe to cook for, and she eats like a bird most of the time," she smiles, but it falters as thoughts of her daughter fill her mind.

"It's ok," Craig reaches a hand out to cover Carly's, "she's going to be just fine."

Nodding, Carly turns her hand under Craig's and folds her fingers around his. "I know. I know. Her letters say she's got herself a little job and that she's happy, in her own way. But I can't help worrying about her, Craig. She's my girl, after all, and I've never felt such a distance between us."

"You know, she could be living somewhere nearby," Craig offers, trying to make Carly feel better.

"I know, and I've told myself that over and over, but it doesn't seem to make any difference," she tells him sadly. "She's gone. Zoe is gone and I don't know if she'll ever come back!"

Giving her hand a squeeze, Craig considers their options. "We could hire someone to find her? I mean, I've never used a private detective before, but I know they're out there if you want to hire one?"

For a moment Carly seems to brighten. The thought of taking some positive action is very tempting. But would it be what Zoe wants?

"No." Carly shakes her head and tries to put Zoe's needs before her own. "She'll come home when she's good and ready, and not before. I know my girl, if I push at her now she'll only move further away from me. I have to trust in our bond to bridge the gap and pray it won't be long before she comes home."

Connor is waiting for her outside the florists when Zoe gets off work.

"Climb in, gorgeous," he grins when she opens the door to look in.

"I can walk home, Connor," she tells him with a sigh. "I'm just pregnant, not disabled!"

But he ignores her, waving his arm to tell her to get in.

"Oh, ok," she grumbles with a smile that renders it moot. "I'm going to have to walk home by myself when your holiday finishes," she reminds him, then watches his smile fade.

"I'm not going back," he tells her. "I have another week at the big house then I'm going to take a place here in the village somewhere. I'm not leaving you, Zoe!"

Not knowing what to say, Zoe reaches over her shoulder and straps herself into the car. "You can't just give up everything and move to Cornwall," she tries to reason with him. "I mean, what about your new business – you can't just let that all go!"

"My business is portable – I can take care of it from wherever I am at the time," he tells her firmly.

"But, Connor..." shrugging, Zoe tries to put her thoughts together. "We need to talk. This kind of relationship isn't something we can enter into lightly."

"Lightly," he repeats. "You think I made the offer to look after you and the baby, lightly! I've never been more serious about anything in my life!"

Her mind and heart are in turmoil. Her head is telling her to give Connor a chance, that he's different now that she's getting to know him.

But her heart still belongs to Palmer.

"I appreciate that, I do," Zoe asserts quietly. "But I can't turn my feelings on and off like a tap. I still love Palmer, Connor. You need to know that and accept that it will take time for my feelings to change."

If they ever do...

As if he'd heard her thoughts, Connor gives a disgusted groan. "I'll drive that man out of your heart for good. He never deserved you, Zoe. Just give me a chance to prove I can be good for both of you, that's all I ask?"

Considering him long and hard, Zoe eventually nods and Connor gives a whoop of joy.

"You won't regret this," he tells her, pulling away and driving with care to the house he is still renting. "I'm taking you to my place – we may as well use it until the rent is up."

"You want me to stay there with you?" Zoe asks, somewhat alarmed.

"Of course! Look at it like a holiday, make the most of the pool and the excellent view. And by the way, it has an outdoor Jacuzzi that we could use tonight," he suggests, and laughs when her eyes go wide.

"Let's live a little," Connor suggests. "Tonight I'm taking you out for dinner and then we're going dancing!"

"What! No. Connor, I'm pregnant!"

"But you're not dead. Enjoy it while you can – having a

kid is going to cramp your lifestyle soon enough," he tells her.

"Won't it cramp your lifestyle if you take us on as you suggest?" she asks curiously.

"Of course, but that's my choice – you don't really have a choice now, do you?" Connor states frankly.

"I have a choice, and my choice is motherhood," Zoe states just as frankly. "I could still have an abortion if that's what I wanted."

"But you won't – you don't have a cruel bone in your body, so let's not pretend you ever had a choice!"

He's right! And not because of who I am, but who the baby's father is. I still love Palmer, and if having this baby is the only good part of him that I get to keep, then so be it!

"It isn't real," he says. "The man you think you love doesn't even exist. He conned you just like he conned my parents and everyone else who called him friend. You can't love a figment of his imagination. It was all a lie!"

Her bottom lip trembles and her eyes instantly fill.

All those tender moments – the times we made love and gave ourselves to each other – were they all just playacting. I don't know that I can accept that.

"What we have can be so much better," Connor tells her. "We start off honest and build on that foundation.

You and me, Zoe, we can make a life for *our* child!"

That does it! That declaration opens the flood-gates.

"Connor..." Her hands cover her mouth, and tears fall so fast that they flow over them.

"You're mine, now Zoe. You, me and our child will be a family. A real family!"

Later that evening, Connor takes Zoe home to collect a few things, but tells her that he's taking her shopping the next day.

Getting ready in the Hollywood style bathroom, is so surreal that Zoe has a fit of the giggles. *This is all so crazy!*

But the night out is just what she needs. Dressed in her best, Zoe knocks Connor for six. He's so proud to be stepping out with her on his arm. And he makes her feel so special.

The nightclub is stomping, the music loud and they lose themselves in the dancing.

Connor glares at anyone who even looks at Zoe like they're going to try to cut in. And Zoe is made to feel beautiful and wanted again.

She's been on her own for so long. Has wanted to feel loved and cherished, but her dreams were shattered. Now Connor is helping her to rebuild them, bigger and better than they ever were before. For there is a child involved this time, and Connor has offered them both a future.

He really cares! It may not be true love that binds us – not yet. But it could be, one day, if we give what we have now a chance to grow.

That night they spend their first night together. By choice, she gives herself to Connor and he loves her well.

In the morning, the bright sun of an early spring summer wakes Zoe from an exhausted sleep. They had stayed out until the early hours of the morning dancing, and then had made love for a long time after that.

Now her body feels limp and sated, though her heart still aches for what she has lost.

We can do this. You can do this, she tells herself. The baby deserves to have a father, and Connor couldn't have been kinder or more gentle when he loved me last night.

Getting up, Zoe walks out to the swimming pool and looks across the sea sprawled out for miles in front of her. Then she dives into the water and swims to her heart's content.

"So, you did go skinny dipping after all," Connor laughs when she finally swims to the side of the pool. Holding a hand down towards her, he helps Zoe climb from the pool.

Standing naked before him, Zoe feels suddenly shy.

Drinking her in, Connor's eyes move over her glistening body. He watches as water drips from her nipples and runs in rivulets down her lush body.

"Here." Taking a large soft towel, he wraps it around Zoe and pulls her in, holding her naked against him with the towel. "You are stunning. It would be worth renting this place all year round just to see you get out of the pool that way."

"And you're a pervert," she laughs self-consciously, and takes the corners of the towel out of his hands to wrap it more securely around herself. "But I can understand why you rented this place. It's beautiful, isn't it," she says, turning to the early morning sun glistening on the sea out to the horizon.

"Yes, beautiful." But Connor is looking at Zoe, content to have captured her beauty for himself.

I knew I could. And now I'm going to make sure I keep her, and her child. Mine!

Palmer has gone over his failed tenders with a fine toothed comb, and can find nothing unusual about them.

His margins were all reasonable, as low as he could make them to ensure that his men were kept in work through this lean time in the building trade.

In any trade! The damned economy has gone to hell, but we should have won at least one of these tenders, even going on the law of averages.

But we didn't, and I want to know why!

A couple of the new, more experienced office girls were now covering his secretarial needs. And the more experienced of those was keeping his diary.

"Mandy, can you come in here," Connor buzzes through to the outer office.

"Yes, Mr Johnson, how may I help," she asks primly.

No matter how many times he's asked her to call him Palmer, Mandy always calls him Mr Johnson.

"Do you have a key to this filing cabinet?" And he points to the three drawer unit at the side of his desk.

"I don't believe so, sir," Mandy tells him. "But I'll go through the keys in my desk and see if I can find one. Is it locked? I could telephone a locksmith if you need to get into it," she offers.

"No, that's fine. But do have a look for a key, I want it in my possession from now on."

He doesn't even really know why. It's just something niggling at the back of his mind, and he wants to cover all the bases.

"Never mind, I'll order a new one!"

"A new key?" Mandy asks confused.

"No, a new filing cabinet!"

Once his mind is made up, Palmer goes on line to search out the most secure cabinet he can find. Then he orders it and pays extra for next day delivery.

He has new tenders to submit for some very large jobs and he intends to take them home with him until the new, more secure cabinet arrives.

He works late into the night. If he doesn't get more work soon he'll have to start laying off men just to keep the rest ticking over with the contracts that he already has on his books.

Pulling out his mobile, Palmer calls his friend and foreman. "Craig, I need a meeting with you at my place tomorrow night," he tells the big man. "You can bring Carly, but she may get bored. We need to go over the tenders we lost and the ones that I'm planning to put in — I want your input before this company sinks out from under us!"

Craig agrees and they arrange to meet straight after work.

"Carly won't mind," Craig tells his boss and best friend. "She's a reasonable sort. As long as I let her know I won't be there for dinner, she'll be fine with it."

"How's that working out for you," Palmer asks, referring to Craig's continuing relationship with Zoe's mother.

"She's a lady," is all Craig says. Then he chuckles deeply, "And she's the best damned cook on the planet. I swear I'm in food heaven!"

They laugh, and Palmer is happy that his friend has finally found happiness with a good woman. "Well, I'm in hell, as far as this business goes." He could have added that he was in hell as far as his private life, too, but he refuses to let his thoughts go there.

"Hmm," Craig's deep brown voice rumbles over the telephone. "Something isn't right about all this. It just isn't right!"

"I agree, but we'll talk about it tomorrow, ok?"

"Ok."

Palmer stays up until his thoughts begin to blur and his eyes start to close of their own volition.

With his head on his pillow he begins to fall into sleep. *It isn't right. Something isn't right!*

<u>CHAPTER NINE</u>

When the new filing cabinet arrives, Palmer transfers all of his sensitive documents into it and locks it securely.

He's really impressed with the build, it looks strong and the lock is first rate.

Now we'll see what we see. Something has been going on that I'm still not sure about, but if no one can get at the tenders in advance then they can't undercut them!

And it would be interesting to see who won all those contracts that I suddenly didn't? Was it one company, if so I'll find out who and what connection they have with my company. Because somebody must have been feeding them my confidential information – whether it came from this office or from the submissions office, I will find out who and where!

When Craig arrives at Palmer's flat that evening, he is alone.

"Carly didn't fancy the boredom then," Palmer chuckles when he greets his friend.

"No, said she'd rather read – I did say that she could do that here. But she said she's been on her own for a lot of years, one more night isn't going to make any difference."

Then Craig sees all the tenders and other paperwork splayed out over every flat surface. "You've been busy. Got any ideas?"

"Yes," Palmer frowns, "and no."

They cross to the dining table where Palmer has an A4 pad that he's been making notes on.

"That's when things started going haywire," and he points to the date and name of the first contract that he didn't get. "I've been over the tender I put in for it, and there's no reason I shouldn't have won that contract. But you can't win them all, right?"

Craig nods, his eyes roving over all the figures and they seem reasonable to him, too.

"But then I went over all of these other tenders that weren't successful, and not one of them has anything about it that is unusual or overpriced," Palmer tells him with a sweep of his arm to indicate the stacks of paperwork he's got laid out.

"So, you're thinking sell-out?" Craig frowns down at the list that Palmer has put together and has to agree. "Sounds reasonable, but who and how?"

"I don't have a clue about that yet, but I do know who's been benefitting from my sudden run of bad luck," Palmer glares at Craig, his anger evident in his glinting blue eyes.

"Who...?"

"Henry Snelson! His company has won all but one of the contracts listed here," Palmer tells him. "So now, he's climbing up in the construction league, where as he was virtually falling out of it before this happened."

"So you think he's got a mole in your office, or the submissions office?" Craig's deep voice has a nasty growl to it.

"I do! We have a lot of new staff at the office, but it started before Zoe left," Palmer reasons.

"You're not going after Zoe on this...?" Craig asks angrily.

"No! Damn it, stop getting all defensive, I'm just mapping out the timeline," Palmer assures his friend. "We need to work out who had the opportunity, and none of the new staff that came in after Zoe left are relevant."

"But the one's she hired prior to leaving could be," Craig points out.

"Yes, exactly. Now we need to do a background check on all of them and see if they have any connection to Henry Snelson or anyone at his company."

Frowning deeply, Craig asks, "How the hell are you going to find all that out? You can't exactly walk up to them and ask – they wouldn't tell you the truth anyway."

"No," Palmer agrees. "But there are people who do this work for a living. Investigators who have ways and means that we know nothing about."

"I talked with Carly about hiring one of those PI's," Craig admits. "We were talking about Zoe, and I thought it would be a good way of finding her."

"But Carly didn't agree...?"

"No, she wants to let Zoe come home when she's good and ready. Sorry," he adds when Palmer's face falls.

"It's driving me crazy," Palmer declares suddenly. "I'm trying to sort this lot out and all the time I'm thinking about Zoe! Where the fuck did she go?!" Palmer demands loudly. "Her father won't even acknowledge my letters – he told me on the day she left that 'he'd seen it with his own eyes', apparently referring to a couple of photos that Zoe showed him. But how the hell can anyone photograph something that never even happened? Craig, I've thought about it over and over, I never met up with an old girlfriend, or any other damned female!"

"Could it have been staged?" Craig asks quietly, trying to think of any likely scenario.

"Staged? I suppose so, but why, and how would they make it look convincing enough to fool Zoe and her father?"

Craig stands up to his full height and stretches even further. His muscles are tight from a hard day's work and he rotates his shoulders a few times to relax them.

"Got a beer?" he asks as he walks away from Palmer to stand at the floor to ceiling windows.

Palmer moves to get the big man a drink and hands him an opened bottle, keeping one for himself.

When Craig turns from looking out over the city, his eyes are narrowed and focused on Palmer. "Could be that all this is connected. All the trouble you were having with Zoe, her leaving, and your business being driven into the ground! Could be you have an enemy you aren't aware of!"

Stopping with the bottle almost to his mouth, Palmer stares at his friend in amazement. "You think someone set this all up from the start. Everything!"

"I think it's highly probable," Craig nods. "And if you really think about it, you'll see there's one person who stands out from everyone else!"

Sudden dawning has Palmer's jaw dropping open.

"You're kidding! I know he hates my guts at times, but he's my brother. No way would Connor pull a stunt like this!"

Craig takes a mouthful of beer and swallows thoughtfully. "You've said yourself, Connor wants whatever you've got. Did he ever show an interest in Zoe?"

"Damn it! It can't be! He wouldn't!"

Would he? For christ's sake, I must be crazy even thinking along these lines. But it would make a macabre sense. Connor! You bastard!

Craig can see when the penny falls into place and just nods.

"But how has he been getting into the office to get at the tenders?" he asks Craig. "He was working for you at the time – did you notice him go missing off site?"

"Not once," Craig confirms. "If he accessed the office, he did it out of works time!"

"But the office is locked up and alarmed at the end of the day," Palmer reasons.

"So who could get him access?" Craig asks, already knowing the answer.

"Laura! She's head over heels for Connor, I'll bet she would have done anything he asked," Palmer speculates.

"They looked pretty tight at the works barbecue,"

Craig recalls. "Though, it looked a little one sided to me."

"Yep. Laura has always been more taken with Connor than the other way around," Palmer acknowledges. "He's always been a jerk with women."

"So maybe you need to have a word with Laura. Could be she's been copying the tenders for him to sell off to Snelson."

"Jesus!" Palmer scrunches his hands in his hair and squeezes till it hurts. "I can't believe I didn't see this before. Connor – it's starting to make sense."

"You were hurting before," Craig says quietly. "Your mind hasn't been straight since Zoe left."

Slumping down onto a settee, Palmer puts his head in his hands.

That's an understatement! My guts are twisted up so bad I can barely eat or breathe. For christ's sakes Zoe, couldn't you have trusted me. Couldn't you have at least asked me about the photos before you took off?

"I need a proper drink," he states, putting the beer bottle down on the coffee table. "You want one?" he asks, having crossed the room to the kitchen area and holding up a bottle of whiskey.

But Craig shakes his head, knowing he has to drive home later.

"I'm not sure you should either," he tells Palmer, concerned for his friend.

"Don't worry, I'm not going to sink into oblivion at the bottom of a bottle," Palmer sneers angrily. "But I do need a drink."

With that he pours himself a small tumbler of whiskey and takes a good swig of it.

"I'm not giving up on Zoe, and I'm not going to stand by and watch my company go belly up," he states, slamming the now empty glass down on the work-surface. "If Connor is behind all this, he'd better find a damned small rock to crawl under, because if I find him, I'll kill the bastard!"

At the doctors, Zoe has her first antenatal examination and is relieved when she's told that all appears to be going as it should.

Her dates are confirmed and Zoe is given the due date for her baby.

"September 21st," she tells Connor, her smile so bright and wide it is dazzling.

"Boy or girl," he asks, his excitement pleasing Zoe no end.

"He couldn't tell me that, silly," Zoe laughs. "I have to have an ultrasound scan for that."

"So when do you get to have one of those," Connor frowns, thinking the whole thing sounds really long winded.

"He made an appointment for me for May 9th, that's about 3 weeks away," she tells him. "They should be able to confirm my dates and maybe even tell me the sex of the baby. Only, I'm not sure that I want to know."

"What! Of course we need to know," Connor gasps disbelievingly. "How can we plan the baby's room if we don't know what it is? I mean, imagine if we paint it bright pink and it's a boy – we could damage the little man for life!"

Laughing hysterically, Zoe is enjoying Connor's involvement. "But wouldn't it be exciting to wait – to just be told on the day 'you have a little boy, or a little girl'," she asks softly.

"No. No, I think it would be more exciting to give the little chap a name – like, I wonder how Oscar's doing today. Did Oscar keep you awake last night?" he tries out the sound of it.

"Oscar? No, if it's a boy I was thinking more along the lines of Andrew, or Liam," Zoe suggests with a hand over the roundest part of her stomach.

"I suppose," Connor agrees with a frown. "But what if it's a girl?"

"Hmm, I can't decide..." Zoe muses.

"Brook," Connor says instantly. "I've always loved that name."

"Brook Johnson – I suppose it does sound pretty neat," she smiles. "Brook Johnson it is," she states happily.

"But Andrew – he'll get called Andy for sure," Connor muses with pursed lips.

"Liam then," Zoe suggests. "If it gets shortened to Lee it'll still sound nice."

"Ok then. Brook or Liam Johnson – I'm really looking forward to being a dad!"

But it should have been Palmer who helped me decide the names. And he should have been looking forward to being a dad.

Some of her introspection must have shown, as Connor pulls her into his arms and kisses her soundly.

Think of me! Only of me! I can make you happy. I can drive him out of your heart for good! Just think of me!

"Let's go shopping! There must be lots of things we can buy that aren't necessarily for a girl or a boy?" Connor wants to distract Zoe, to get her to let him in on the preparations for the baby.

"There are so many things we'll need," she laughs. "And we will have to get one of the bedrooms at the cottage prepared, even if we just clear it out and paint it cream."

"That's what we'll do then," Connor agrees happily.

"We'll buy decorating supplies as well, then I'll get started on painting it!"

With a hand to his cheek, Zoe looks into Connors excited eyes. "Thank you. Thank you for making this a special time. I thought I would be doing everything on my own."

"You're not on your own, anymore," he tells her, and turns his lips into her palm to kiss it. "I'm here to stay."

CHAPTER TEN

Laughing, Zoe uses a paint rag to wipe off the smudge of paint that Connor just put on her nose.

"I'll get you back for that," she tells him, but he ducks out of reach and she just stands with hands on hips.

"You'll have to be quicker than that," he tells her, laughing as she tries to catch him. But as she goes one way, Connor goes the other until Zoe has to give up.

"If I weren't nearly five months pregnant I'd catch you," she tells him with a happy grin.

"Not on your life – girls are too slow," he teases. "Let's hope we're having a boy, then I can teach him how not to let the little girls catch him – until he wants them to, of course."

It doesn't jolt so much when he talks about them as a

couple having a baby. Not now that Connor has actually moved in with her and they are living together.

It had seemed stupid for him to get a place of his own when the rent was up on the big house in Millendreath. But he had offered, and that was the main thing.

Now they are looking forward to tomorrow and the ultrasound of the baby.

"You still want to find out the baby's sex," she tells him, when he catches her and holds her to him.

"Be honest, wouldn't you love to get to know our son or daughter a little better," he asks. "We have months to wait until we meet them, but they don't have to be a stranger the first time we hold them," he tells her convincingly.

"What a lovely thought." Zoe sinks into his arms enjoying the solid feel of being held safe and warm by a man who loves her.

Tipping her head up to look at Connor, Zoe smiles, "If it means that much to you, we'll ask. Ok?"

"Yeah! Then we can really decorate this room," he tells her excitedly.

"And you won't mind if it's a boy or a girl?" she asks tentatively.

"Not on your life – if it's a girl I'll give her running lessons so that she can outrun the boys that'll be after her if she takes after her mother!"

The worst part about going for an ultrasound is the need to have a full bladder.

Zoe has been struggling recently with frequency and urgency, so deliberately filling her bladder and then forcing herself not to go to the loo is nothing short of torture.

"I swear I'm going to wet myself if they don't take me in soon," Zoe complains as she watches another young mum go in before her.

"Just go," Connor tells her. "I bet they won't even notice."

"No, they will," Zoe tells him earnestly. "You see that woman at the back with the red top on – I saw her come out about 20 minutes ago and they brought her a large pitcher of water and a glass then told her to get drinking. I heard the nurses say that she must have been to the loo recently as they couldn't see a thing!"

Pursing his lips, Connor gives her hand a squeeze in support. "Looks like you're going to have to keep your legs crossed and locked together then," he chuckles and Zoe bats him with her free hand.

"Don't make me laugh, you idiot. If I wet myself I'll blame you!"

"Zoe Benson," a voice calls from further up the small corridor. "Zoe Benson," it repeats.

"Yes, yes I'm here," Zoe calls out, not wanting to miss her turn.

"Ah, right this way," the young woman smiles. "And is dad coming in too," she asks when Connor hesitates.

"Come on, dad, I can't hold myself for much longer," she smiles at a chuffed Connor.

After helping her to lie on the bed, the ultrasound operative lifts Zoe's top to expose her rounded stomach.

"This might be a bit cold," she warns, as she squeezes some clear gel onto Zoe's tummy then puts the probe into it. "The gel helps us to get a better picture and the probe to move easily over your stomach.

"Now watch that screen," the operative tells them, pointing to a small monitor. "I'll tell you what to look for when I find your baby."

Then suddenly, a small shape comes on screen and Zoe clutches Connor's hand, her other hand flying up to cover her mouth.

"A baby," Connor states, stunned and stupefied.

"Yep, that's what it is alright," the Sonographer agrees with an indulgent smile. "Now then, do you want me to try to tell you the sex of the baby?"

Zoe looks up at Connor; his face is transfixed on the screen.

"Yes please," she confirms quietly, not wanting to

break the spell that Connor appears to be under.

Moving the probe on Zoe's stomach, the Sonographer describes the various parts of the body while taking a myriad of measurements.

"Ah, that's pretty clear, I think," the Sonographer smiles brightly. "A little girl, do you have names?" she asks indulgently.

"Brook," Connor answers before Zoe can think. And she settles back to watch the wonder of fatherhood settle over Connor.

"She's beautiful," he tells no one in particular. "Brook Johnson – you're going to be lovely, just like your mum!"

Connor squeezes the hand he is still holding, and turns to smile down at Zoe.

"A girl – we're having a daughter!"

"Yes. Brook Johnson. I think we should pick a middle name out for her," Zoe suggests.

When they get back to the cottage, Connor won't let Zoe do anything. It's as if seeing the baby on the ultrasound screen has made the pregnancy even more real for him.

"I'm not sick, Connor," she pleads when he suggests she give up working at the florists. "And I like my job, it gives me another outlet, a place where I meet people and get to talk to them."

"But you've got me now. And you don't need to work, I'll take care of everything," he offers brightly.

"And I love that you want to do that for us," Zoe tries to reason with him. "But I need a life outside of this cottage."

"And what about when the baby's born, you won't be working then, will you?"

"No, but I'll have Brook to keep me busy."

Zoe can't put her finger on why she is so reluctant to give up work. It isn't that she couldn't find plenty of things to occupy her time. But it would be isolating, and she doesn't want to become solely dependent on Connor for conversation and social interaction.

I know you want to be everything to us, but I need more. And I need time to adjust. You're not Palmer – no matter how hard you try to be!

When Grady calls later that night, Connor is still brooding about Zoe's reluctance to give up work, and the fact that she won't let him take care of her.

"So, what else have you found out?" he asks when Grady gives him his daily report.

"I got a bit more on Hickey's past criminal record and the work he does for his boss, Jennings," Grady tells him, sounding pleased with himself. "More than one person has gone missing after meeting with Hickey. And I mean missing, as in never heard from again."

"Jesus! I knew that creep was dangerous, but I'll still take him out after what he did to me!" Connor declares quietly. Angrily.

And not just because he all but bashed my brains in, I could forget about that. But putting me in Palmer's debt – I'll kill him for that alone!

"I also found out something you might be interested in about Snelson. He's had dealings with Jennings. More than once he's taken financial help from Hickey's boss."

"So, Snelson is in bed with Jennings – interesting. Keep digging, I want to know if he's still in debt to him, and if so how much. I want everything you can find out about Hickey, Snelson and Jennings. Just don't let anyone get a sniff of the fact that you're looking into them, or you'll suddenly disappear never to be seen again," he warns.

I might need to pay Palmer's office another visit! I've only got one more tender to pass off to Snelson and I need more money!

At breakfast the next morning, Connor tells Zoe that he needs to be away for a couple of days. "I just need to meet up with a couple of clients and then I'll be right back."

Zoe sucks in her bottom lip and tries not to worry.

"Yes, ok, that's fine. We'll be fine. But hurry back, ok."

"Will you stop looking so worried," Connor smiles, reaching across the table to take her hand. "I'll be back, and if I run into Palmer I won't say a word about seeing you. Right?"

Nodding, Zoe realises that this, more than anything, is what is worrying her. Feeling guilty, she overreacts by getting up and giving him a fierce hug.

Connor's heart all but explodes in his chest. He loves that Zoe is accepting him into her life more and more.

"I'll be right back, ok?"

"Ok."

When he kisses her, Connor can feel his pulse race and his need for her builds instantly in his loins. But since he's seen the baby inside of her for real, he is hesitant to take her as he wants to.

"I'll bring you something nice back with me," he tells her, cupping her cheek in his gentle hand.

"You don't have to do that," Zoe tells him, kissing him again then holding him close. "You've already done so much for us, I don't really understand why."

He pulls back to look into her eyes, his own soft with love. "I do it because I love you. There, I said it. Now stop brooding and thinking up even more things to worry about. We're going to be fine. You, me and Brook. We're all going to be fine together!"

"Ok," she smiles, a little relieved that he hadn't expected her to tell him she loved him in return. It is too soon after Palmer for her heart to belong to anyone else. But she does care for Connor. She cares for him very much.

"I'll miss you," she tells him instead.

And that appears to be enough, if his goofy happy grin is anything to go by.

The long drive back up to Birmingham gives Connor time to think.

"Grady, I've arranged a meet with Snelson at the usual place. I want you there but I want you out of sight, unless I give you the nod," Connor tells him over the speakerphone.

"Yes sir. Are we meeting up prior to that or should I give you my report now?"

"Anything interesting?" Connor asks.

"Oh yes, I think you would call it that," Grady gives a rasping chuckle. "Snelson not only had loans from Jennings, he had to sell over half his business to him to get him off his back when he couldn't pay up."

"What!" Connor explodes. "You mean to tell me, that it's Jennings I've been helping to screw my brother?"

"That's about the size of it," Grady replies.

"Fuck! That is not what I intended at all." And Connor

has to contemplate what to do next. "This is going to be the last deal I do with Snelson – what he tells Jennings is up to him. My deal has always been with Snelson."

"Not sure Jennings will see it that way, as he owns more than half of Snelson's company," Grady points out in his low growl.

"Does Jennings know you're on to him?"

"No sir! I know how to keep my tail covered," Grady tells him confidently.

"Ok, keep it that way. I've booked into the Holiday Inn, as usual. Meet me there at 7 sharp. My meeting with Snelson is at 8, so that'll give us plenty of time to go over a few things."

For the rest of the journey, Connor chews over his conversation with Grady.

Jennings! He must have a finger in just about every worthwhile business pie in Birmingham, and God knows where else! Why the hell did he have to be involved?

This could get sticky. I wanted to bring Palmer down, but if Jennings is involved it could get a lot more serious than that. And what would Zoe think if she found out I was involved in getting Palmer hurt?

He couldn't even bring himself to think the word 'killed' because it made him feel sick to the stomach. He was in over his head and he knew it. Unwittingly he had put his brother in danger, now he had to figure a way out of it.

All during dinner in his suite, Connor thinks about what he is going to tell Snelson. It is different now that he knows he is really dealing with Jennings, but he doesn't want Snelson to know that he knows the score.

I'll just play it as usual. The slug can buy me a few drinks and I'll give him the last tender, then I'll tell him the gravy train is going off the rails. The deal is done, finished, over. And he can make of that what he chooses!

Sitting in the hotel lounge, Connor sips on a double whiskey and watches Snelson slither into the room.

As he walks towards Connor, he sees the overweight man put a finger in his too tight shirt collar and run it around his neck.

So, you're nervous, Snelson. Why is that, I wonder? Have you had a run-in with Jennings? Or are you running up gambling debts again?

"Take a seat," Connor tells Snelson when he draws level with him. Then he crooks a finger at a nearby waiter. "A double whiskey, and whatever he's having – and he's paying," Connor adds with a sneering grin.

Henry Snelson doesn't argue, but sits and puts his briefcase by the side of his chair then undoes his suit jacket buttons.

"Connor," he greets the younger man. "Haven't see you around for a while – have you moved?"

"That would be none of your business," Connor tells him coldly. "But this is," and he holds out an A4 envelope with the copy tender in it.

Deciding not to ruin the meeting right from the off, Connor sits back to enjoy his drink while Snelson takes a discreet peek in the envelope.

"Ok, our usual deal," Snelson says, putting the envelope in to his briefcase and taking a fatter one out of it.

He leans forward to pass the small package under the table to Connor. There are only a few people in the lounge, and the exchange goes unnoticed.

"Make the most of that – it's the last one," Connor tells him.

"What?! We have an arrangement – you can't back out on it now!"

Snelson's face has taken on a purple colour, a decidedly unhealthy look for the overweight man.

"Get over it, Snelson. You've had a good run, and if you've learned anything from the tenders I've already given you, then you should be able to keep winning at least a few of the contracts that you bid for!"

"You can't do this! He'll kill me!"

"He...?" Connor asks, knowing full well who Snelson is referring to.

"Jennings – he's a small time hood who has his greedy hands in my business!" Snelson gulps down his drink then holds his glass up for the waiter to get him a refill. "You don't just walk away from his type."

Laughing, Connor stands and puts a hand to Snelson's shoulder. "Good luck with that!" And he walks away without a backward glance.

CHAPTER ELEVEN

Palmer is working hard in his office. He's having to work all the hours God sends to pull back some of the work he's lost out on.

He's been out looking at prospective jobs, large and small, anything to keep his men working.

Craig has been working hard alongside him, with Carly encouraging him to help his friend out of a jam.

She really has been supportive, considering that Craig's boss was once her daughter's fiancé who she ditched at the altar for apparently cheating on her.

That still didn't sit well with Craig. He knew that Zoe wouldn't have gone off like that without some pretty damning proof – be he also knew his boss and best friend.

If any man was a dyed-in-the-wool faithful husband

type, it was Palmer. Now if it had been his brother, Connor, Craig wouldn't have doubted his guilt for a second.

That kid can get himself into trouble before he even takes a step out of bed! He's just fucked up every which way he turns!

"So, how many jobs have you got lined up to put a tender in for?" Craig asks Palmer as he looks through the plans for a new high-rise office block due to be built in Leicester.

"I've already sent out quotes for three smaller jobs – they won't start for between 6 and 8 months. Which is about when the work will start to get a little lean," Palmer tells him, rubbing his stubbly chin.

"And the bigger stuff...?"

"I've got one tender in for a job worth £3.75 million, and another almost ready to go for a job worth £1.2 million," Palmer sighs heavily. "If I get either of those it will help steady the ship for a while, but I need at least a couple more to make it smooth sailing again."

"Ok." Craig's soft brown voice rumbles out as he nods his head. "Ok."

"What does Carly make of all this – is she hoping I'll sink without a trace?" Palmer asks with a wince.

"Don't be thinking like that," Craig reproves him.

"She's a kind hearted lady who is just looking out for her daughter. But no, she doesn't wish you anything but good luck. And, if you ask me, I don't think she believes you were cheating on Zoe," Craig states with a firm nod of his large head.

"What makes you say that? Has she heard from Zoe? Has Zoe had a change of heart too?" he demands, his mind going into overdrive.

"Carly gets letters from Zoe on a fairly regular basis," Craig begins to tell him, then holds a restraining hand up when Palmer makes to dive in with a lot of questions. "They are posted to her father in America firstly, then he posts them on to Carly. Zoe really doesn't want anyone to know where she is living," Craig states firmly. "I told Carly, and I'm telling you, she could be just around the next corner just needing to keep her head down for a while. There's no saying where she is, but at least we know that she's alright."

Palmer is pacing the floor, thoughts of Zoe being nearby driving him crazy. "I love her, Craig. I need to find her and put this all straight and as far behind us as possible."

"But you still don't know who set you up in the first place. Wouldn't that be the smart thing to concentrate on?" Craig asks calmly.

"Damn it! Why are you always so logical? Don't you have a flaming heart?" Palmer demands hotly.

"I do, and it's hurting for all three of you," Craig tells him. "I see first-hand how badly this mess is affecting at least two of you; I can only imagine how badly it's affecting Zoe, too!"

"You're right. As soon as I get this business back on its feet, I will find out who's been sending those letters!"

"That sounds like a good idea. Have you seen or heard anything of Connor lately?" Craig asks, trying to change the subject.

"Not a thing. Which is worrying as hell seeing as he can't keep himself out of trouble for more than five minutes," Palmer states wearily.

"I asked Laura if he's been in touch, but she said no. Apparently he didn't even have the decency to tell her they were over – just disappeared and never bothered to get back in touch."

Craig shakes his large, round head. "Did you ask her about the tenders?" But he can see by the uncomfortable look on his friend's face that he hadn't.

"She was really upset over Connor...and what difference would it make now?" he shrugs. "If Connor talked her into copying a few tenders for him, he's the real culprit. She's just his gullible stooge," Palmer sighs sadly. "But I'll be keeping a very close eye on her, you can be sure of that!"

Nodding and pursing his lips, Craig keeps his thoughts on the matter to himself and instead asks, "What about your mother, has she heard from Connor?"

Letting out a hiss of anger, Palmer says, "She's worrying herself silly over him! Jesus, couldn't he at least phone her," he asks Craig, slamming his hand down on the kitchen table. "Wouldn't you think he'd have enough sense to know she's worried sick over him!"

"You know Connor better than that," Craig laughs out loud. "That boy doesn't do anything unless it has some benefit to him. He wouldn't expend the energy it takes to breathe if it weren't for the fact that it keeps him alive!"

Palmer can't help but agree. "Ok. You're right. This is Connor we're talking about."

But I can hope, can't I? I'm actually worried about him myself. He just dropped out of sight after he finished working for me — which I knew would happen someday soon. I just hadn't expected it to be so final!

Where the hell are you Connor, and what are you up to?

Henry Snelson is having a hard time telling Jennings that the deal with Connor Johnson has come to an end.

"He said he can't get anymore, that that's the last one

and we should move on," he tells Jennings over the speakerphone.

"So, he wants out does he!" The line goes quiet and Snelson starts to sweat. "I suggest you tell him to think again – I say when the deal is done. Have you been paying him the money we agreed?" Jennings asks accusingly.

"I have. I have," Snelson pleads. "I don't know why he's pulling out, but we can hardly force him to do anything he doesn't want to. It's not like we have anything on him."

Again the line goes quiet and Snelson begins to think they've been cut off. "Hello..."

"You tell him, if he doesn't continue with our deal I'll be taking a personal interest in his brother's welfare – do you understand me, Snelson?"

"I do, yes Mr Jennings, and I'll certainly do my best," he tells him as he wipes the sweat from his brow with a handkerchief.

"You'd better, or I'll be asking Hickey here, to take a personal interest in your welfare!"

And after hearing Hickey give a cruel laugh, the line really does go dead.

"Oh God! Oh Jesus! I'm a dead man!"

An hour later and Snelson finally gets through to Connor.

"We need to meet," Snelson tells him without preamble.

"I'm leaving in the morning, we don't have anything more to discuss," Connor dismisses abruptly.

"Your brother's life depends on it. Now stop pissing around and meet me at the hotel tonight at 8pm," Snelson snaps out, surprising Connor and cutting the phone connection.

What the fuck? So...Jennings is trying to play hardball. Well, we'll just see about that! He hasn't got anything on me, not since my benevolent brother paid my debt off.

But he decides to meet up with Snelson to find out exactly what is going on.

"Grady, I want you in the hotel lounge at 7:30 tonight. We'll have a drink then you'll move into the shadows while I talk to Snelson," he tells the obedient PI.

"No, I have no idea, he just said my brother's life depends on this meeting," he tells Grady when he asks what it's all about. "I'll go along with it for now, but they've got nothing on me."

Then why are you so worried? Grady asks himself when he hangs up.

The Holiday Inn lounge is noisier than usual. A small convention has booked in and is making use of the lounge for a meeting place.

Just before Snelson is due to arrive, Grady slinks out of sight to observe the meeting.

Snelson looks like a dead man walking when he finally arrives. He's had to struggle through some late evening traffic and is none too pleased to see Connor relaxing with a drink like he hasn't a care in the world.

"Johnson! Do you have any idea what kind of trouble we are in?!" Snelson demands as he takes a seat opposite Connor.

"We? I think not!" Connor sneers contemptuously.

"Yes, we!" Snelson affirms stonily. "Jennings is spitting nails over you backing out on our deal. So you'd just better think again!"

"I don't have a deal with Jennings – you do," Connor states categorically. "If he's got a problem with anyone, it's with you. Nothing whatsoever to do with me!"

"Are you really that naive?" Snelson asks. "A man like Jennings doesn't make that kind of distinction. The way he sees it we had a deal for you to supply me with copies of Palmer's tenders, now he's expecting you to continue doing just that!"

"I never said I'd do it indefinitely. If you told Jennings any different, that's your problem," Connor grins acidly.

Laughing, Snelson just shakes his head. "Who do you think you are? This isn't the playground where you get to run away from the bully — in this case the bully will not only catch you and stick your head down the toilet he will kill you then bury you beneath it. Literally!"

Connor actually pales at Snelson's descriptive words, knowing exactly what Hickey is capable of.

"I never broke my word, damn it!"

A nearby crowd of people turn to see what the raised voices are all about, and Connor pulls himself together quickly.

"You tell Jennings that he can go fuck himself. I don't owe him anything," Connor states, more confidently than he actually feels.

"Oh I'll do that. You can just bet your life I will. Then I'll sit back and watch the shit hit the fan and see just who gets covered in it — 'cause it won't be me. I can tell you that much!"

No, you damned creep! It won't be me either. I think it's time to take care of a little problem named Hickey!

Connor spends the next couple of hours talking on his mobile to some pretty seedy friends from his past.

"I'll give you 5 grand a piece just for doing what you love. This creep needs the crap kicking out of him — if he ends up in the hospital, so much the better," Connor tells the leader of the men he's been talking to.

"Right then, I'll get back to you with the details,"

Connor smiles after getting his willing agreement, and shoves his mobile back in his pocket. "They can't wait to get started," he tells Grady, who actually doesn't look too enamoured with Connor's plan.

"Are you sure this is the best way to go?" he dares to ask. "I mean, if Jennings even suspects your involvement, it could come back on you big time!"

"I won't even be in the city – how can I possibly have anything to do with Hickey getting a kicking," Connor laughs hideously. "And besides, the man has so many enemies it could be anyone!"

"Right," Grady agrees, though his brain is telling him to steer clear of this mess.

At midnight, Connor goes out to the seedier side of Birmingham to meet up with the goons he's hired to do Hickey over.

"Ok, you get half now and half when it's done. My man will give you the second payment when I know for sure that Hickey's in the hospital," he tells the men, who all look like they are strung out on something that you can't buy from your local chemist.

It's cold and dark on the streets of Birmingham, but that isn't what is chilling Grady to the bone.

He's been working for Connor for a few weeks now, and he's finally worked out what he's been delivering and getting paid for.

But this is different. This is taking his PI job into goon territory, somewhere he'd never planned to go.

Maybe it's time to move on? Things are starting to come unglued, and more than a little dangerous. I think I'll wait for my next payout then cut and run.

CHAPTER TWELVE

Looe is enjoying some pretty good weather and has a lot of visitors. The florist shop where Zoe works is busier than ever.

"Hi, how can I help?" Zoe asks a white haired lady who is looking a bit lost.

"Thas awright my ansum, am jus lookin roun," the woman says with a broad Cornish accent that makes Zoe smile.

"You're obviously a local, do you live in Looe?" she asks, enjoying the woman's friendly demeanour.

"Naw, I live in' Saltash, but a wus born an bred in Looe," the woman smiles at Zoe warmly.

"Ah, so you're a visitor today then," Zoe declares. "I won't disturb you, if you want to browse."

After walking around for a few minutes, the woman comes back to the counter and brings with her a beautiful vase that is for sale.

"A like 'at," the woman declares. "How much 'ed it cos to av it filled with en arrangement like that un?" she asks, pointing to one of the silk flower arrangements on the back shelf. "But real flowers, mind – I dun hold wi em things."

"Hmm, would you be wanting to take that with you today?" Zoe asks with a thoughtful frown.

"Na good ta me ere, is it my ansum," the woman grins cheekily. "But am not goin ome till 2ish," she adds helpfully.

Looking at her workload for the day, Zoe grins. "Just for you, I'll stay a little later and get that done. Now, what name shall I put it under?"

"V'ronica Potter," the woman states proudly. "En I'll pay fo it na," she tells Zoe, already pulling out her purse.

When Tara comes in from the wholesalers an hour later, Zoe is hard at work making up arrangements.

"How's it going?" she asks, looking over Zoe's work with a satisfied smile.

"Great, I've taken some more orders – one for pick up this afternoon," she tells Tara with a grin. "A lovely lady who was actually born here but now lives in Saltash – you should have heard her accent, it was lovely!"

"How are you doing with the orders for today?" Tara asks while looking over the workbench behind the shop counter.

"Great, I've almost finished those and I'm about to get started on Mrs Potter's order."

"Hmm, it's getting near your knocking off time...," Tara observes. "I might have a job finishing it off with the wedding I've got to start on this afternoon."

Smiling broadly, Zoe shakes her head. "Not to worry, I promised Mrs Potter I'd stay and do it myself – I don't mind, really."

"Well, I'm not going to refuse the help," Tara says, grateful that Zoe is flexible with her time. "If it's alright with you, I'll pay you the extra hour or so rather than you taking the time back. We're inundated with orders at the minute."

"That's fine. In fact, if you could use me I wouldn't mind putting in some extra hours," Zoe offers brightly.

"Is that man of yours still away?" Tara asks, having been careful not to pry in the past.

Zoe blushes and looks down at the flowers she's working on. "Yes, I didn't think he'd be away this long. It's been over a week now."

"Is it business?" Tara asks casually, but watches Zoe carefully.

"Yes, though he can take care of most things from here – I think he had to go for some meetings, or something," she adds with a frown.

"Hmm, not thinking of leaving us, are you, Zoe?" Tara asks concerned.

"Oh, no," Zoe declares quickly. "No, not at all. I love it here!"

"Well, that's good. Because I would hate to lose you," Tara tells her while heaving a sigh of relief. "Now, about your hours, you tell me what you'd like to work and I'll sort it out and let you know what's what!"

Grinning happily, Zoe nods. "That sounds great! I get so fed up on my own at the cottage – I might as well be at work where I get to meet the most interesting people," she declares.

Looking out of the shop window, Zoe watches the multi-coloured crowds of people, milling about outside and occasionally wandering in for a browse.

She loves Cornwall, with all of its quirks, and the local people who are characters all in themselves.

By 2 in the afternoon, Zoe has put the finishing touches to the arrangement for the local lady who'd wandered into the shop that morning.

What a woman! Not one I'd like to cross, but friendly enough to be sure. And I did love her accent, so very...Cornish!

"I was just thinking about you," Zoe chuckles as Veronica Potter herself walks into the shop. "I have your arrangement for you."

Turning to pick it up off of the back workbench, Zoe places it on the counter.

"Well, my ansum, thas grand," Veronica smiles in delight. "Jus as I imagined it."

Zoe's grin widens with pleasure, delighted to have gotten it right. "Do you have a car nearby?" Zoe asks, concerned for the woman who isn't too steady on her feet. "I can carry it out for you, if you'd like?"

"Eee, yor a good gel, but ey's fine. My son's on front wi the car," Veronica assures her.

"Then let me just carry it out for you," Zoe tells her, taking the arrangement off the counter and walking with the woman out to the car.

Feeling much better once she's seen Veronica safely out to the waiting car and handed her the arrangement to hold in the front seat, Zoe waves goodbye and goes back into the shop.

Removing her apron, she clears away the flower cuttings and other equipment then wipes the surfaces down.

"That's enough for today," Tara tells her, having come in from the back room. "You get off now, and if you feel like coming back in the morning I could more than use your help."

Smiling happily, Zoe agrees to come in on what is usually her day off to do some extra hours. It gets lonely at the cottage without Connor, now that she's grown used to having him around.

When Connor has time to think about what he's done, he begins to regret setting David Hickey up for a kicking.

Being with Zoe has changed his outlook, and he realises how stupid he was to let Snelson wind him up.

But what's done is done. I'll just have to keep my head down and get back to Zoe. Jesus, I can't believe I've been back for more than a week. I hate this damned city!

Deciding to do one more thing before heading off back down to Cornwall, Connor calls in on his mother.

Climbing out of his car, he isn't surprised to see her planting more flowers in the front garden and walks up quietly to surprise her.

"Hi, mum," he grins mischievously.

"Connor!" she gasps and fights her way to stand up. "Connor, where on earth have you been? I've been sick with worry about you," she tells him, and bats his arm with a muddy hand.

"Hey, if you're just going to beat me up I'll stay away," he jokes, but Dorothy doesn't let him move away from her.

"Oh, Connor," she weeps, wrapping her arms around her sons waist. "Why do you always cause me to worry? I've missed you so much."

Wrapping his arms about his mother, Connor gives her one of his rare hugs. It doesn't seem so hard to do since he's learned more about loving someone from Zoe.

"Take it easy, you'll crack my ribs if you hold on much tighter," he warns with a laugh.

"Come on in. Let me have a look at you," his mother tells him, wiping her eyes on a clean patch on the back of her hand.

He can't remember his mother being so glad to see him before. *Perhaps I should stay away more often!*

"Here now, you sit down and I'll make you a nice cup of tea," she offers, moving about the kitchen and putting the kettle on.

"I'd prefer a cup of coffee," Connor tells her, but happily takes a seat in the conservatory to look out on the bright summer's day.

"You've done wonders with this garden," he tells her. "Are those marigolds over there?" he asks when she brings in a tray of drinks with a plate of cake and biscuits.

"They are," she frowns at him curiously as she hands him his mug of coffee. "Connor Johnson, will you tell me what is going on? I have never known you to ask about the garden, let alone be able to tell me the name of any of the flowers?" she tells him with a purse lipped frown.

"There's nothing going on," he tells her innocently. "But, I suppose it might have something to do with the fact that I've met someone that I want to settle down with."

"What! When did this happen – and why haven't we met her?"

"You haven't met her because we live too far away – but she's the best thing to ever happen to me. I love her, mum. I really do!"

Her eyes fill and a hand flies up to cover her mouth as Dorothy takes in her younger son's news. "I'm so happy for you, darling. But won't you tell me about her – couldn't you bring her to meet us and maybe stay here for a few days?"

"She's pregnant mum – it wouldn't do her or the baby any good to travel all the way up here," Connor smiles indulgently.

"Pregnant! Connor, you can't expect us not to want to meet her – she's carrying out grandchild, for heaven's sakes."

"I know, I know. And when the time is right, I'll bring them both to meet you all, but not just yet, ok."

"But..."

"Just give us some time to work things out then, I promise, you can meet her and you'll be able to spoil your granddaughter," Connor laughs when his mother's eyes go wide and round.

"A granddaughter – you know it's a girl?" she asks excitedly.

"We do," he grins. "So get your knitting needles out, she's due about half way through September – just in time to enjoy Christmas!"

"Oh! Oh my heavens!" Dorothy cries, her hands shaking when she tries to drink her tea. "I'll get started right away. She'll need cardigans for the winter, and blankets for the cot, and maybe a few pairs of bootees and mittens too!"

Laughing at her enthusiasm, Connor can only wonder at his mother's reaction. He really seems to have pleased her at last.

"I'm going to get back to them tonight," he tells her. "I've already been away for a week."

Getting to her feet, Dorothy whirls around the kitchen gathering up things for him to take home with him.

"Here, now, I've put some cake that I made this morning in here," and Dorothy hands him a round cake tin. "And there's some nice fresh veg that your dad dug out of the garden just yesterday – she'll need lots of fresh veg to keep her and the baby healthy," his mother tells him fussily.

"Mum, we're fine. She gets to eat lots of fresh food from around where we live," he tells her. "Now I'm going to get off or I'll hit the tea-time traffic."

Throwing her arms around his waist again, Dorothy buries her head in his chest.

"I'm so glad you came to see me – I'm just sad that your dad wasn't here," she cries, her tears falling unheeded onto his shirt front.

"Come on, mum. You don't usually take on like this when I leave," he tells her with a frown.

"You don't usually disappear for weeks on end," Dorothy scolds as she dries her eyes. "And don't you take so long to visit next time or I'll have something to say about it, Connor Johnson!"

He knows his mum is angry when she uses his full name, but she's back to hugging him again so he can't be in too much trouble.

"Ok, ma," he jokes, and grins when she bats his arm again. "I'll be back up to see you in a few weeks, so stop worrying. Ok?"

When Dorothy waves her son off she is full of pride and confusion.

Why on earth won't he bring her to meet us, or even

tell us anything about her? Damn it, Connor – why do you always have to make me worry about you?

Dorothy goes back to planting in her garden, her heart lifted by the joyful news her son has brought her and happy in the knowledge that he is safe and happy too.

CHAPTER THIRTEEN

The crowd around the man's body is buzzing with morbid excitement.

Someone has beaten a man beyond recognition, and to within an inch of his life.

The sirens blare into the night sky, the warning lights from police cars and ambulances causing an almost Northern Lights effect across the front of nearby buildings.

"Ok, people, stand back please," an officer yells, his arm trying to move them physically away from what is a crime scene.

"Get some light over here," one of the paramedics calls out, and a police officer obliges with a torch until better lighting can be facilitated. "That's it, hold it right there!"

"Hello, hello, can you hear me...?" the paramedic shouts close to the man's ear. But he gets no response.

His fingers are already on the man's carotid artery feeling for a pulse.

"Amazingly, he has a pulse but its faint and thready. We need to blue light him to the hospital, fast!"

With great care, the man's neck is stabilised and his limbs secured. Any sites of obvious bleeding are padded and he is loaded into the back of the ambulance where I.V fluids are commenced.

The concrete where he'd laid is now thick with blood and cordoned off for police investigators to get started on.

"Do you know the man who was just taken to the hospital?" An officer asks one of the crowds of onlookers.

But no one seems to know him or to have seen anything happen. He is a mystery – yet another on the police records waiting to be solved.

Grady is hiding in the shadows, his cheeks pale and his heart racing. He'd seen the beating. He'd been the one to call the police and the ambulance, but he hadn't dared to come forward.

He is getting out of the city tonight, and he won't be back any time soon. If the man dies he could end up hip deep in trouble, maybe even prison, and that isn't worth any kind of money!

Connor is on his own now!

When Palmer looks through his records and those of the builders who won the contracts that he felt he should have won, one name keeps cropping up.

"Snelson," Palmer tells Craig after handing him a drink and taking a seat on the settee opposite his large foreman. "He hasn't won every one of the contracts that I lost, but he won most of them!"

"Hmm," Craig contemplates the mug of coffee in his large hands, "yet he was losing most of what he went for prior to your tenders inexplicably missing the mark so many times. Doesn't sound right, does it?"

"No, it doesn't," Palmer agrees. "It damned well doesn't. There's something fishy going on, I just don't know how to prove it!"

"Do you think he somehow bribed the selection process?" Craig asks, his brows knit in consideration.

"Maybe. But it's not like he could just bribe one person – they weren't all city contracts. Some of them were private companies looking to expand or to build new premises. Who the hell would he bribe then?" Palmer asks, his hands rising then falling helplessly into his lap.

"I don't know – but it doesn't seem logical that a man who couldn't win a big contract for years, suddenly comes good with his recent tenders, does it?"

"I have to agree — there's something else going on here. Something that we haven't thought of," Palmer tells Craig. "But it definitely has something to do with Snelson — he's at the back of all this. I just don't know how!"

When the landline rings it actually makes both men jump, so deep are they in contemplation of the problem.

"Hello, Palmer Johnson," Palmer answers abruptly.

"Mr Johnson, this is Staff Nurse Emily Bretton of the Critical Care Unit at Queen Elizabeth Hospital, Birmingham. Could you please tell me if you have a brother?"

"What! Yes, I have a brother — why do you want to know?" Palmer asks, alarmed beyond thinking clearly.

"Mr Johnson, could you please tell me the name of your brother?" the Staff Nurse asks.

"His name is Connor Johnson — now please, tell me what this is all about?!" he demands hotly.

"I'm sorry to have to tell you, that we believe a young man who was admitted to this Critical Care Unit just an hour ago, may be your brother, Mr Connor Johnson. If that is the case, we need you to come to the Queen Elizabeth Hospital, Birmingham as soon as possible and as a matter of urgency!" the nurse tells him.

Pushing his free hand back through his hair and gripping the roots tightly, Palmer has to make himself think! "Why can't he tell you himself who he is?"

A brief silence screams down the line, then the nurse tells him, "Because the man we are treating isn't able to communicate with anyone. He is on a ventilator and is in an extremely critical condition, which is why we need you to get to this department as soon as possible."

"Connor...?" Palmer can't believe his ears. "Connor is in Critical Care?"

"Yes, Mr Johnson," the nurse reiterates patiently. "I cannot urge you strongly enough to make the journey here immediately."

It takes only seconds for the chill of understanding to flood his veins. "I'll be there in 20 minutes, and I'll be bringing our parents."

Putting the telephone down, Palmer can only stare at it.

"If I got the gist of that conversation right, we had better get a move on," Craig tells him. "I'll drive you to pick up your parents then drop you all off at the hospital. It'll be quicker than you trying to find a parking space and a lot safer. You're in no fit state to drive," he tells Palmer, just in case he has any ideas about protesting.

But Palmer doesn't protest. He climbs into Craig's car in a stupor, his mind reeling and struggling to make sense of it all.

"Mr and Mrs Johnson," Craig addresses the boys' parents at their home, "I need you to come with us to the hospital. It's urgent," he tells them when they look back at him blankly, "they rang just a bit ago to say that Connor is critically ill and needs you there asap – I'm here to take you."

After a brief moment of shock and disbelief, the Johnson's climb into the back of Craig's car and he ferries them all to the hospital.

"Palmer, do you know what's going on?" his mother asks, a note of restrained panic in her unnaturally quiet voice.

Shaking his head, Palmer turns in his seat to look at his parents. "I don't know anything more than you do – the hospital just said it was imperative that we get there as soon as possible."

The atmosphere in the car is strained and strangely quiet; no one daring to ask the question that is on everyone's mind.

Will Connor still be alive when we get there?

The large building is lit up like a Christmas tree against the night sky, and the A&E department looks as busy as usual.

Craig drops the family off and tells them that he will be in as soon as he can park. Then he leaves them to find Connor.

"Excuse me, we're looking for the Critical Care Unit," Palmer tells a receptionist.

After getting concisely delivered directions, Palmer and his parents rush to Connor's side.

The unit is a scary place to be – all manner of alarms and signals are beeping and ringing and nursing and medical staff are responding in a calm, organised fashion to them all.

A Staff Nurse asks if she can help them, and her eyes struggle not to show concern when they tell her who it is they've come to see.

"If you would like to follow me," she tells them, guiding them to a separate room, "I'll just get Connor's doctor to come and explain what is going on with his treatment."

Only a couple of minutes pass before the doctor comes into the room, but it had felt interminable.

Holding out his hand to each of them, the doctor introduces himself then takes a seat opposite.

"I understand this is the first that you have heard about Connor being in the hospital," he says, watching them nod in agreement. "Then I know it must have been a shock and I'm sorry for that but we needed to get you here as fast as we could."

"That's what the nurse said," Palmer chimes in. "But

what she didn't say was what is wrong with Connor – why is he in the hospital in the first place?"

Frowning and nodding, the doctor takes the time to quickly align his thoughts then ploughs in with what he knows will be devastating news.

"Connor was found badly beaten on a street somewhere in Birmingham – the police will be able to give you more details about that," he offers with a grim smile. "He was rushed here and has already been to surgery where his numerous injuries were treated." He stops, looks at the devastated faces of his patient's family and knows that they have even worse to listen to.

"Beaten...?" Dorothy Johnson's eyes are confused when she turns them to look at Palmer. "I don't understand...he was going home...he shouldn't even be here...are you sure it's Connor?" she asks hopefully, turning to look back at the doctor. "Are you sure it's Connor Johnson? Our Connor Johnson?"

The doctor nods his head sadly. "I'm afraid there is little doubt. He had identification on him and he is a match for previous medical records that we hold for him."

"But you can't know for sure if he isn't able to talk," Palmer states hopefully. "He might have had someone else's wallet or documents, or whatever the hell else they used to identify him," Palmer tells the doctor angrily.

Holding his hand up to calm him, the doctor addresses Palmer's concerns. "Your brother has a couple of scars on his body that exactly match the medical records for Connor Johnson, but if you would like to make a formal identification that would be helpful."

Nodding, Palmer stands ready to do just that, obviously hoping that there has been some tragic mistake.

"It would be best if we do this alone," the doctor tells the parents, and turns to leave when they nod in agreement.

As they walk towards Connor's room, the doctor stops Palmer to prepare him for what he is about to see.

"This patient has suffered serious upper body and facial injuries that have necessitated the use of extensive bandaging and therefore you will not be able to see his face," the doctor warns. "However, we have noted the scarring, as we just talked about, and would ask that you make your identification on any markings that you might recognise as distinguishing marks."

Palmer nods, he understand what the doctor is saying and begins to prepare himself for the worst.

"I think you should also know that this patient is on a ventilator which is doing his breathing for him via a tube that goes directly into the trachea," and the doctor indicates a point at the base of his throat. "It wasn't possible to ventilate him orally due to the extensive facial injuries."

Standing outside the side-room door, Palmer steadies himself then enters the room to face what needs to be faced.

No matter what the doctor has told him, Palmer isn't prepared for the sight that greets him.

With a sheet folded back to his waist, Connor is undeniably lying in a hospital bed all broken and still, the only sounds coming from the ventilator and a monitor above the bed.

Tears splash down Palmer's cheeks unheeded, his hands going out to touch his brother but not daring to make contact.

He looks at the naked chest before him, purple with bruises and various deep grazes. Then he sees the scar he got when he was a boy having fallen out of a very tall tree and he turns to nod at the doctor, then turns back to Connor.

"What the hell happened?" he asks his brother. "Who did this to you?" He knows that Connor can't answer, but still he needs to voice the questions tearing at his heart. "Why didn't you come to me – if you were in this kind of trouble, why didn't you come to me?"

His voice is getting louder as his anger rises. "You

stubborn fool, I would have done something...anything..."

The doctor puts a calming hand on Palmer's arm and gives it a gentle squeeze.

"We need to go back to your parents now," the doctor reminds him. "They need to know for sure."

Nodding, Palmer moves to stand at his brother's side then bends to speak into his ear.

"I love you, bro. Don't let go, you can beat this thing if you try hard enough. Now live, damn it!"

Returning to his parents, Palmer has to watch his mother crumple into his father's arms when he nods to confirm that it is their son lying next to death in a hospital room.

Having waited for the storm to pass, the doctor takes the time to go into more detail about Connor's injuries and the treatment he is receiving.

"I want to be able to say that everything we are doing will bring Connor home to you," the doctor tells them sadly, but shakes his head. "However, I need to be honest with you," and he looks from one to the other, making sure that they are all listening to his next words. "Connor's chances of survival are extremely slim, and if by some miracle he did so it is almost certain that he would do so with considerable brain damage."

Dorothy lets out a smothered scream, then bursts into inconsolable tears in her husband's arms.

CHAPTER FOURTEEN

Oh my Lord, what a wonderful day! The sun is shining and the river looks so blue and radiant. I couldn't ask for a better start to the day.

After putting some fresh bird seed on the bird-table and some more nuts out for the squirrels, Zoe goes back indoors to get ready for work.

It has been manic at the florist shop, and she is now working five mornings a week, and staying a little later when needed.

What with all the weddings, and the inevitable funerals, they have been run off their feet trying to fill orders.

But Tara isn't complaining. And neither is Zoe, really. It's actually quite satisfying work, an outlet for her creative bents.

Taking her time now that her pregnancy is progressing, Zoe walks the short distance to work.

On arrival she finds Tara already hard at it, with buttonhole flowers lined up on the bench and ready to put into a delivery try.

"They're lovely," Zoe smiles when Tara looks up to greet her. "What time did you come in this morning?"

"I was up at 5 and started work at 6," Tara grins as Zoe cringes at the thought.

"Thankfully, we were still tucked up in bed," Zoe tells her, holding a loving hand to her very round belly.

"Is Connor back yet?" Tara asks with interest.

Shaking her head and frowning, Zoe puts her handbag in the back room then comes back to talk to her boss.

"It's strange...he usually calls at least once, if not twice a day – but for the last couple of days he hasn't called at all."

"That is strange," Tara agrees. "Have you tried calling him?"

Again, Zoe shakes her head and takes a seat near to where Tara is working, picking up a flower to help turn it into a wedding buttonhole.

"I don't like to," she says quietly. "I know he has to go to lots of meetings – I might embarrass him if I call in the middle of one."

"But you're worried, right?" Tara asks.

Pursing her lips, Zoe nods again. "I suppose. I just don't want to over-react and cause him any bother."

Thoughtful, Tara concentrates on binding the flower she's holding then puts it in a tray with the others. "Call him. You'll only worry yourself sick if you carry on like this, and I'll bet he'd be glad to know you've missed him."

Suddenly Zoe smiles, then gives a little laugh. "You're right. I'm just being daft – I'll go and do it now," she tells her. And gets up to go out to the back room.

"Well that didn't take much convincing," Tara teases, and laughs while continuing to bind up flowers.

She is just getting a fresh tray when she hears Zoe cry out.

Palmer finally has to go home from the hospital. He got Craig to take his parents' home last night, after they'd had a chance to sit with Connor.

But he'd stayed, sat by his brother's bedside the whole night.

The solitary room had seemed to close in on them. Just him and his brother, nothing else mattered.

He barely noticed the nurses taking care of Connor's needs. Didn't hear the doctors when they asked if he was alright.

Just him and his brother, there was nothing else.

Then a nurse had patted his arm, had given him a bag of Connor's belongings, and he'd signed to say that he was taking them home.

But none of it sank in. There was only him and his brother, the rest of the world could wait!

When he had finally had to leave, Palmer had been loath to go. But the doctors were insistent that it was for the best, at least for now. There were things that they needed to do and they had insisted that he needed some rest.

But it should have been him and his brother, he wanted nothing else.

When he walks into his loft apartment, Palmer barely notices his surroundings. He should fall into bed; he hasn't slept for countless hours. But he doesn't.

Instead he slumps onto a settee, the bag of Connor's belongings dangling from unfeeling hands.

The buzzing noise tries to push its way into his conscious thoughts, but Palmer numbly ignores it.

But the buzzing gets louder, the vibration more insistent, until Palmer finally realises that it is coming from the bag of belongings that he is holding.

Rummaging through the clothes and shoes, he finally finds Connor's mobile, then sits dazed and shocked looking at Zoe's name on the screen.

It isn't until he realises that it must be Zoe calling Connor's mobile that Palmer presses the key to answer.

"Hello..."

"Connor! Well it's about time, I was beginning to think you'd run off and left me!" Zoe laughs then sighs happily.

"Zoe...is that you?" Palmer asks, his voice thick with shock.

"Palmer? Oh my God! What are you doing with Connor's phone?" she asks, stunned to be talking to her ex fiancé.

"Zoe, you need to listen to me," Palmer begs, terrified that she will hang up on him. "Connor's been hurt, he's in the hospital...hello...Zoe are you still there?!"

Tara runs into the back room of the shop having heard Zoe cry out and just in time to catch her before she faints to the floor. Her mobile has already fallen from her hand and she is pale as death itself.

"Zoe," she gasps as she helps her young employee to sit on the floor. Then she hears a voice coming from the nearby mobile. Picking it up, she eyes Zoe warily then speaks into the phone. "Hello, is that Connor?" she asks hurriedly.

"No," the voice on the other end replies, "I'm his brother, Palmer. Is Zoe there, what's going on?" he asks anxiously.

Zoe is staring blankly into space, her eyes shedding tears that she isn't even aware of.

"I think Zoe's gone into shock – what the hell did you say to her?" Tara demands angrily.

"My brother is in the hospital, he's in a critical condition. Can you tell me where you are so that I can come and get Zoe?" he asks hopefully.

Not knowing that she shouldn't, Tara tells him her address and says she'll be taking Zoe home with her. Palmer thanks her for taking care of Zoe then rings off to begin the long journey down to Cornwall.

Three and a half agonising hours later Palmer pulls up in front of Tara's home and climbs out of his car. He's broken every speed limit along the way. But he's here now.

Six months ago, he and Zoe should have been married. Now he's come here to tell her that Connor is dying, and he doesn't know why.

What has Connor got to do with Zoe? How have they kept in touch, and why?

These and a million other questions, have tortured Palmer on his journey down to Looe in Cornwall.

Now he will find out the answers!

Knocking on the door, Palmer stands back to see it opened by a young girl of around 8.

"Mummy," she yells, while looking at Palmer curiously. "There's a strange man at the door!"

Tara comes up behind the girl immediately. "Yes, can I help you?" she asks.

"I'm Palmer Johnson – we spoke earlier," he reminds her.

"Yes, yes, you'd better come in," and she steps back to allow him entry to her home. "Before you go in I want to warn you, if you upset Zoe any more than she has been, you'll have me to answer to, alright?!"

Her eyes penetrate his with unwavering intensity, until he nods and she moves to guide him into the sitting room.

Zoe looks up at him from a chair on the opposite side of the room, her eyes red rimmed and swollen.

But she isn't crying for me, she's crying for Connor. I don't know what the hell is going on. But I know I still love her.

"Zoe." He crosses the room and crouches down in front of her. "Zoe, are you alright?"

Her bottom lip trembles and a tear plops heavily onto his hand. Then his arms are around her and hers twine about his neck.

For a long moment they just hold on, needing to feel the warmth of another caring human being.

"Please tell me he isn't dead," Zoe cries into Palmer's neck.

"He's still hanging on," Palmer draws back to look at her. "But we need to go, Zoe."

Looking up at Tara, she watches her boss nod and knows that she understands completely.

Zoe has confided everything to her friend, and Tara has offered to keep her job open for as long as she needs to be away.

"You get off and see your young man," Tara tells her quietly. "And don't forget to let me know how things are going," she adds ominously.

When Zoe stands, Palmer gasps in shock. He hadn't noticed her rounded shape when she had been sitting, but now her pregnancy is undeniably evident.

Her hand flies to her stomach protectively, and her head rises defiantly, but Zoe says nothing.

Getting over the shock, Palmer takes her elbow to guide Zoe out to his car, waiting while she says goodbye to her friend.

"I'll call," she tells Tara, then finally climbs into his car.

The journey home is just as long but twice as tortuous as the one he took to collect Zoe. Palmer is struggling to come to terms with Zoe's present condition and the fact that she appears to be carrying Connor's child.

When did they even get to like each other? They couldn't stand each other the last time I knew. At least, Zoe couldn't stand Connor – had he succeeded in changing her mind?

Well, obviously – but when and how? Is he the real reason that she left me at the altar? Had she been seeing Connor behind my back?

For fuck's sake – and she was accusing me of being unfaithful!

His mind is working overtime, and hasn't stopped even by the time they pull up in front of the hospital.

"I'll park the car and come up with you," he tells her when she opens the passenger door to get out.

But Zoe silently shakes her head, closing the door before she turns to walk in through the hospital doors.

By the time Palmer reaches Connor's room, Zoe is sat by his bed her head laid next to his lifeless hand, her fingers curled around Connors'.

Pulling up a chair to the opposite side of the bed, Palmer watches transfixed as her fingers move gently over his brother's hand.

He can't feel angry. In fact, he hasn't been able to feel much of anything since he picked Zoe up from her boss's house in Looe.

There is only confusion, for Palmer now.

A couple of hours later a nurse lays a gentle hand on Zoe's shoulder and says, "You need to get something to eat and maybe a drink. This isn't good for you or the baby."

But Zoe just moves her head from side to side, her fingers never stopping the stroking movement on Connor's hand.

"Ok. I'll give you another hour," the nurse tells her. "But at least let me get you a cup of tea and some biscuits?"

Moving her head in a silent nod, Zoe continues her vigil at Connor's side.

Half an hour later, Dorothy and Bill Johnson arrive having stopped off at the church along the way.

When they walk into the room Dorothy gasps at the sight of Zoe sitting with Connor, but Palmer ushers them both outside quickly.

"What's going on? What is Zoe doing here? Does her mother know she's back?" Dorothy asks in a whirl.

"I don't know if Carly is aware that Zoe is back – I only picked her up this afternoon," Palmer explains. "And the last thing on my mind was telephoning Carly – though I suppose I should have," he concedes, his hand pushing back through his dishevelled hair.

"But why is she sitting with Connor?" Dorothy asks, her eyes alight with confusion.

Ushering them to the room they had been taken to by the doctor the night before, Palmer explains everything he knows.

"So, have they been living together do you think?" Bill Johnson asks his elder son.

"I don't know, dad, but it would seem so," Palmer speculates. "And she's really upset. The nurses have tried to get her to take a rest, but she won't leave his side."

Dorothy looks up at Palmer, can see his pain and knows it runs deep.

"Is she pregnant?" Dorothy asks, astonishing the two men in the room.

"How did you know?" Palmer asks, stunned beyond belief.

"Connor told me the last time he visited me at the cottage," she tells them. "The day he was supposed to be going home – the day this all happened," she cries, her hand covering her mouth and her eyes tearing up to blind her.

"Then you knew..." Palmer accuses.

"No. I only knew that Connor was living with someone he appeared to be very in love with and that they were looking forward to having a baby girl."

"A girl..." Palmer repeats stupidly. "They're having a girl."

"It would seem so," Dorothy dries her eyes on a tissue then pushes it back into her pocket. "Now, let's go and see Zoe. She must be beside herself with grief."

Palmer and his father watch her leave the room with her spine held ramrod straight and look at each other and nod.

If she can put on a brave face, then so can they, and they follow Dorothy Johnson back to Connor's room.

As they enter, Dorothy looks at the tea and biscuits left untouched on a table beside Zoe.

"You need to eat something, sweetheart," she tells Zoe, stroking a hand over the younger woman's hair. "Would you like me to call your mother, Zoe? I'm sure she would want to be with you."

At last, Zoe raises her head off the bed and turns it to look at Connor's mum.

"I'm so sorry," is all she manages to say, then the women are in each other's arms and both are crying hot tears of grief.

When they eventually pull apart, Bill hands them a handy box of tissues discretely provided by the nursing staff.

"You need to come home with us," Dorothy whispers quietly. "We can come back in the morning, but you and the baby need some rest."

Zoe makes to protest, but Dorothy won't hear of it. "My son wouldn't want you to put your health at risk like this. You should have heard him when he told me about the baby. He was so proud," she tells Zoe, her eyes filling with fresh tears.

"He told you?" Zoe asks, her eyes going round with shock.

"Just a couple of days ago – right before he left to go home to you," Dorothy smiles. "I've never seen Connor look so happy; you gave him that," she tells Zoe, patting the younger woman's hand with gratitude.

<u>CHAPTER FIFTEEN</u>

Once Zoe has eaten she takes herself off to the guest room Dorothy had shown her when they got home from the hospital, and climbs exhausted into bed.

Her dreams are chaotic, frantic and terrifying. More than once she wakes, sweat on her brow and shaking with fear.

But downstairs they are unaware of Zoe's plight. The Johnson's are trying to puzzle out what is going on.

"That's ridiculous, Palmer," his mother scolds. "Zoe would never have seen Connor behind your back. She was happy, for heaven's sake. Looking forward to getting married!"

"Then how come she's 6 months pregnant with Connor's child?" he demands heatedly, forcing his voice to remain low enough so as not to disturb Zoe.

"I don't know," Dorothy admits. "But I do know that Zoe doesn't have a deceitful bone in her young body. There's more to this than we know, but that doesn't mean to say that she cheated on you!"

Getting to his feet, Palmer begins to pace the sitting room of his parent's cottage.

"I always knew that Connor wanted her," he states eventually. "I could see it in the way he looked and acted around her. And you know he's always wanted everything I had – even as kids!"

Dorothy looks angry, protective of her youngest child who is unable to defend himself.

"Zoe is not some toy that you boys were fighting over. How dare you treat her as such," Dorothy chastises Palmer.

"Now, now," Bill Johnson waves a hand at the both of them, "settle down and lets discuss this calmly." He waits for Palmer to retake his seat then gives them both a warning look. "We don't know for sure how far along Zoe is, and we don't know for sure who the baby's father is," he states wisely. "We are all just going to have to wait for Zoe to give us those answers – but not until she is good and ready to do so," he warns sagely.

"If we go at her like an accusing hoard, she'll up and

run just like she did before," Dorothy agrees with her husband. "I say we give her the time and space to get over what has happened to Connor and the opportunity to tell us herself."

Palmer eventually nods in agreement. "Ok. Ok. I just don't want to lose her again," he tells them sadly.

"It's alright, son, we understand where you're coming from. But right now, we need to concentrate on getting Connor through this mess and support Zoe in whatever way she needs."

"Which should include contacting Carly," Dorothy states firmly. "If I were that girl's mother and I didn't know that she were here, I'd be pretty mad at the people who didn't bother to inform me!"

Again, Palmer nods and says, "I'll go round. If I go now I think they'll still be up."

It is almost 11 o'clock when he pulls up outside Carly's drive. Craig's car is parked on the drive behind Carly's, so he knows the big man is still there.

The sitting room lights are on so Palmer takes a chance on them not minding a late night visitor – especially in the circumstances.

Having knocked on the door, he waits with baited breath for it to be opened.

Now he is here, he barely knows what he is going to

say. Is Carly even aware that Zoe is pregnant? And how do I tell her that we believe the father might be Connor? Or do I say anything at all...?

"Palmer?" Craig's soft brown voice rumbles his name out into the night.

"Hi Craig, can I come in – it's important," he tells him when Craig frowns.

"Who is it Craig...?"

Carly steps into the hallway behind Craig and looks shocked to see Palmer in her doorway.

"For goodness sakes, don't keep your friend at the door," Carly rebukes the big man who is still blocking Palmer's way.

"I hope you didn't come here to upset my woman," his low voice rumbles over Palmer like a badly veiled threat. "I won't tolerate that, not even from a friend!"

Carly blushes at being described as 'my woman', but tingles with joy inside.

"Come on in, Palmer. What can we do for you that couldn't wait until morning? It must be important to call so late," she observes, leading the way back into the lounge.

"I won't beat about the bush...," Palmer begins quickly, "...Zoe is staying at my mother's house and...and she's pregnant."

"What?!" Carly almost keels over with shock, but Craig guides her down to sit on the settee then turns to glare at Palmer.

"What do you mean coming out with something like that?" Craig growls angrily. "Now look what you did!"

But Carly is pulling herself together quickly and her thoughts are racing on ahead.

"Why is she here? And how do you know she's pregnant – did she tell you that?" she asks, not sure why Zoe would confide something like that to Palmer and not her.

"She didn't need to tell me anything," he smiles ruefully, "it's obvious to anyone looking at her. I'd say she must be about 6 months along."

"But...but..." Carly had been trying to stand but has fallen back into her seat again at the news. "That doesn't make any sense. No sense at all. You must have misjudged the situation," she adds hopefully.

Deciding not to argue the point, Palmer merely agrees. "Maybe so. I don't know. But I came to tell you that she's here – my mother was concerned that you should know."

"Then why didn't Zoe come to see me herself? This really doesn't make any sense, Palmer," she tells him, getting more annoyed.

"I only fetched her from Cornwall this morning and she's been at the hospital ever since we got back to Birmingham late this afternoon," he tells her. "As you know, my brother, Connor, is on life support in the Queen Elizabeth hospital – he isn't expected to live," he adds, turning to Craig then rubbing a hand over his tired eyes.

Craig pushes him to sit in a chair before he falls down, then sits beside Carly on the settee. "I think you'd better start at the beginning – this sounds worse by the minute!"

Taking his time, Palmer tells them what has happened since Craig had driven him and his parents to the hospital the previous night.

"They gave me his belongings to take home, and I just sat there holding the bag in my hands when his mobile started to ring." His head begins to shake slowly from side to side as he recalls the moment he saw Zoe's name come up on the ID.

"I just couldn't believe it. It was Zoe calling Connor and when I answered it she thought I was him." He leaves out the part where she'd told Connor how much she was missing him and how she'd asked when he was coming home. It had knocked him for six, and it would only cause Carly more hurt so he keeps that bit to himself.

"I had to explain that Connor was in the hospital and Zoe got really upset. I had to go get her so that she could be with him," he explains, then looks over at Carly to see her reaction.

"Zoe and Connor...?" she asks, stunned by the implication. "But...Palmer, I don't understand?"

Craig slips an arm about her shoulders and pulls her against his strong frame to offer support. "We'll go and see her tomorrow," he suggests. "Then Zoe can tell you all about it herself. I imagine she'll be real pleased to see you."

Carly looks over at Palmer and studies his troubled face. "Will she, Palmer? Will Zoe be pleased to see me?"

He hesitates only a moment, but Carly is quick to draw her conclusion.

"She doesn't know I'm here," he tells her honestly. "My parents and I were talking downstairs and that's when it was decided that you had to be told that she is staying at my parent's house."

"Why didn't she come home to me?" Carly asks, obviously hurt by her daughter's decision.

"It wasn't like that. She wouldn't eat or drink anything at the hospital. Even the nurses couldn't convince her to leave Connor and take a break," he confesses, grimacing at the pain it causes him to admit that fact. "It was only when my mother took charge that she was able to convince Zoe to go home with them and get some rest.

She's tired out and went straight to bed after having something light to eat and drink."

"Well, at least she's being looked after," Carly smiles wanly, holding on to Craig's hand for comfort. "Maybe we could go over to your mother's house in the morning – we could speak to Zoe before she goes back to the hospital to see Connor again."

"Sounds like a plan," Craig agrees with a slow nod of his head. "We'll get some sleep now and be up bright and early to go see Zoe!"

The following morning is bright with sunshine, not in keeping with Zoe's sombre mood at all.

"Are you alright, dear?" Dorothy asks when Zoe walks into the breakfast room. "Can I get you something to eat?"

The last thing Zoe feels like is food.

"Would you mind if I just have a round of toast, I don't think I could stomach too much more," she smiles wanly.

"Go sit in the conservatory," Dorothy suggests. "I love looking out over the garden at this time of day, and I can bring your tea and toast out to you the minute it's ready."

Glad to escape, Zoe nods with a grateful smile. I don't know how to act. How to be around Connor's family. I just want to get to the hospital. Please, God, let Connor be alright. Please.

Seating herself, Zoe watches the birds flit and land on a nearby bird-table and the hanging feeders that Dorothy fills for them.

Then she sees Palmer walk from behind a particularly large bush and feels her heart leap.

Her hand falls to her belly and smoothes over the roundness of it. That's your daddy baby. He doesn't know you yet, but maybe one day he will. If we can just get past all the pain.

Palmer bends to pluck out a stray weed that his usually fastidious mother has missed. He can see Zoe watching him, wishes she would join him, but knows that now isn't the time to try and win her back.

But he wants to. He so very badly wants to tell her to give him another chance. The chance to prove he is innocent of whatever the letters have convinced her that he has done.

I love you, Zoe. I haven't stopped loving you. I just wish you hadn't stopped loving me.

When her mother arrives, Zoe is at first anxious, fearing her mother's recriminations. But Carly soon dispels her fears, wrapping her in the same mother's love that she has showered on her over the years.

"Now, more than ever, you need a mother's help and support," Carly tells her. "And I want to be there for you, now and after the baby is born."

"Brook," Zoe states, her bottom lip trembling badly. "We're having a daughter, and Connor chose her name. She's Brook Johnson," Zoe moves into her mother's arms and cries as if her heart is breaking.

Dorothy turns to her husband for comfort, and Palmer is so damned hurt and confused. To hear Zoe talk about Connor like they are a couple is killing him.

"We'd better make our way to the hospital," he suggests. Looking over at Craig he says, "Can we manage everyone between us?"

The big foreman nods his head, "No problem, boss. I'll help you get everyone over there then I'll get to the Dersinger site and make sure it's going on the way it should. I left Sean in charge; he'd be a good man to think of next time you're looking for a new foreman," he states.

Nodding, Palmer ushers everyone towards the front door and doesn't protest when Zoe climbs into Craig's car with her mother.

"It'll be alright, son," Bill tells Palmer from the backseat. "Zoe's a fine girl – I don't believe anything is quite what it seems," he adds wisely.

Palmer frowns, it all seems pretty plain to him. It is obvious that Zoe is pregnant with Connor's child – he had told their mother that he was going to be a dad just a couple of days ago. And now Zoe turns out to be pregnant and is obviously in a relationship with Connor.

"There doesn't seem to be much doubt about what's been going on," he murmurs, not even realising that he said the words out loud. "Connor is going to have a daughter, Brook Johnson, before too much longer."

Two at a time they are allowed to visit with Connor. It is hard to sit with his brother, but it is equally hard to sit in the waiting room with his parents and the rest of Connor's visitors.

"I brought you a photo of Brook," Zoe tells Connor, sliding the ultrasound photo between his thumb and fingers. "Do you remember how she looks; her thumb is in her mouth already, she won't need a dummy when she's born," she smiles bravely.

"You need to wake up soon, Connor," she tells him while wiping his eyes with a cool damp cloth that the nurse has given her. "These nurses have really sick patients to look after – you can't stay in bed with a few cracked ribs you know."

Zoe doesn't realise that she is no longer alone – Palmer has stepped quietly into the room and hears her one-sided conversation with his brother.

"Being a dad is hard work, and you said you wanted to be Brooks daddy – you need to wake up now, Connor," she insists, her tears adding to the water that is washing the tiny part of his face that is visible between the bandages and dressings.

"He can't," Palmer tells her quietly, watching as she jumps at the unexpected sound of his voice.

"Of course he can," Zoe argues angrily. "He's just resting for a bit, then he'll get stronger and take us home," she states, the hand on her stomach caressing their unborn baby.

Deciding not to force reality on to her, Palmer says instead, "They're giving him a lot of sedation – they're deliberately keeping him asleep to let him heal."

With a bright smile, Zoe turns to Palmer and almost rips his heart out. "That's right! You're right! Did you hear that Connor?" she asks, turning back to Connor's unmoving body. "They just want to keep you asleep for a while to help you heal. Just rest a while longer. We'll go home soon," she tells him, sitting down to hold his hand and lay her head in its usual position on the bed next to him.

The room is silent but for the ventilator and the beep of the monitor.

Connor lays still and unresponsive. Palmer has lied to spare Zoe. The doctors already told him, on their arrival, that all sedation has been turned off to allow them to assess Connor's neurological functions.

He hasn't shown any signs of waking up. Not a blink in response to the doctor's voice, not a jerk in response to pressure or pain, in fact none of the usual responses that the doctors were looking for.

For all intents and purposes, it would seem that Connor has already left them. But they are giving Zoe time to come to terms with that awful reality.

CHAPTER SIXTEEN

"I won't listen to this!" Zoe stands in the room where the doctors often have to give relatives bad news, and where she has just listened to them explain the need to carry out a brain stem test on Connor. "You just don't want to give him the time to wake up. He's just sleeping! He's been through so much, he just needs more time!"

Palmer stands, moving to block her exit from the room. "You have to listen," he tells her, catching her arms and turning her to face him. "Connor isn't going to wake up – he can't," he says, watching the news gradually sink in and seeing the pain growing in her eyes. "I'm sorry, Zoe. Connor's gone – these tests are just a legality, a way of proving beyond doubt what we already know. Connor is gone."

Crumpling into his arms, Zoe cries and moans with the pain of her loss. Then she begins to pummel on Palmer's chest, taking out on him the hurt that is tearing her apart inside.

"You don't care about Connor - you want him to be dead! Why didn't you give him a chance? Why didn't you protect him like a big brother should?!" she demands, her grief turning to insane anger. "Where were you when Connor was being beaten up – were you with another one of your floozies?"

Of all the things she'd thrown at him, that last cut straight to his heart.

"No!" he takes her shoulders and shakes Zoe to snap her out of her growing hysteria. "I was never unfaithful to you – when will you ever believe me!"

"Never!" And with that Zoe tears out of his grasp and returns to Connor's side. *Let them do their tests, then they'll see that you just need more time!*

They allow Zoe to sit with Connor for another couple of hours, then the doctors ask her family to take her home so that they can perform the standard brain stem test.

Instead of going back to Connor's mum and dad's cottage, Zoe goes home with her mother.

In her old room, Zoe texts Tara with the latest news then lays on the bed wrapping her arms around her stomach.

I'm sorry baby, I didn't mean to get upset. I know it isn't good for you when I do. I'm going to rest for a while, you have a sleep too.

Moving her hand to caress her growing stomach, Zoe finally falls into a restless sleep.

When Palmer arrives at the house sometime later, Carly reluctantly invites him in.

"Please, Palmer, I know that what Zoe said was out of line...," Carly tells him as she takes him through to the lounge "...but you saw how upset she was, I don't think coming here was such a good idea."

"I just came to tell you the results of the testing," Palmer grimaces uncomfortably. "Basically, it's what we all thought, Connor has no brainstem function. The Consultant has asked us to come back tomorrow morning for a family meeting – I think they're going to ask us to let them turn off the life-support," he tells them, feeling an iron band of pain constrict his breathing.

"And you think Zoe should go?" Carly asks warily.

"Don't you?" Palmer looks Carly square in the eyes, wanting no confusion on this matter.

"I'm not sure," she tells him, hesitantly.

"Well I'm sure," Zoe walks in with her head held high, her red rimmed eyes telling their own tale. "There's no way I'm not going to be there with Connor. I was there for him when he was happy and looking forward to Brook being born. I will be there for him when his life is ended!"

"Zoe..." Palmer turns to speak to her.

"Get out! Get out and never come back," she tells him, her anger not abated in the least.

"Zoe listen..."

Craig moves forward, holding up a hand to Palmer he guides him out into the hallway. Closing the lounge door behind them, he turns to Palmer. "You know she ain't thinking straight," he tells his friend. "I'll take them both to the hospital in the morning – does 10 o'clock sound about right?"

Palmer nods and moves out of the front door that Craig has just opened for him. "I'll ring the hospital and tell them to expect us about then. I'm sorry if I've upset her again – I didn't mean to."

The drive back to his loft is a lonely one. Palmer wants nothing more than to comfort Zoe, but she won't let him near her. Not physically and not emotionally.

How can I prove my innocence if she won't let me in? How can I make her understand how much I love her, how much I have always loved her if I can't get near her?

And how can she be 6 months pregnant if she didn't cheat on me?

Then a loud bell tolls in his head, the sound of clarity

amidst a storm of confusion.

"She's mine! Brook is mine!" he shouts out into the empty car. "Damn it, Zoe, you can't do this! You can't keep her from me!"

Arriving at his flat, Palmer makes his way up to his loft and paces it like a caged lion.

Somehow he has to win Zoe back. He has to win his family back. Now he's had time to think about it, him being the father is the only thing that makes any sense.

And my dad has already figured this out! Damn it, why didn't he just come right out and say it? I could have let Zoe go back to Cornwall without ever knowing the truth!

But where does knowing get me? Zoe doesn't want to know – I still don't know what the anonymous note writer sent her. Maybe Tara would know? Maybe that's who I have to win over to get through to Zoe?

At the hospital, everyone goes into the family room to have the details explained to them. It is, as Palmer had explained to them the previous night, a meeting to discuss the switching off of Connor's life support.

"If there was something that we could try, anything at all, then we would," the Consultant tells them. "But Connor isn't able to respond to any kind of treatment. Without the ventilator and the drugs we are giving him, he would not be alive. To all intents and purposes, Connor is gone, it is the ventilator alone that is forcing his body to continue to breath."

Although Zoe's bottom lip trembles, she holds back the tears and nods with absolute resolution. "I'm nothing and no one to this family, but if my opinion counts for anything I say we let him die in peace," she tells the room, then stands and walks out of it.

Going directly to Connor, Zoe sits by his bedside and takes his hand.

"I know you can hear me," she speaks into the empty silence. "I couldn't love you the way you seemed to love me, but you already knew that and loved me anyway. But I cared for you deeply, and our daughter will have the name you chose for her." Standing, Zoe moves to kiss Connor's lips through the bandages covering his face.

"You will always be special, you will always be loved, and I will make sure that Brook knows what a great daddy you would have been."

Behind her, Palmer listens with his heart sliced open and bleeding. Then he leaves the room quietly, leaves Zoe to say goodbye to the man who'd been about to replace him in her life.

Going in to work seemed about the only thing Palmer could do after his brother's life support had been turned off.

He'd taken his parents' home, had stayed with them for a little while. But then he'd had to get away from the grief. He'd needed to separate himself from Connor to stop himself from becoming angry.

But it hasn't worked. Palmer is pacing his office with all his emotions so raw and painful that his mind can't seem to keep up.

His thoughts go to Zoe, to the pain she must be feeling and the fact that he can't comfort her.

Then he gets angry at her for getting involved with Connor in the first place. If only she'd told him about the baby – wouldn't that have been the sensible thing to do.

But then, she thinks I've been unfaithful to her. That I'm not worthy of being a father!

With his hands balled at the roots of his hair his voice roars out in anguish.

Without knocking, Craig walks into his office and closes the door behind him.

"Wanna get drunk?" The big guy asks his friend.

"I want to commit murder," Palmer tells him, his fists finally loosening their grip on his hair. "I want to know who is behind all of this. What cretin sent those notes, gave Zoe whatever proof it is that she thinks she has, and who murdered my brother!"

Moving behind Palmer's desk, Craig gets out two

glasses and pours out a couple of very large whiskeys.

"Stop tryin' to think. Today you lost your brother – it's a day for grievin' not thinkin'!"

Taking the glass being offered to him, Palmer takes a huge swig of the amber liquid and relishes the burn at the back of his throat.

"You're right – let's go back to my place and do this properly!"

All evening they drink and blather, blather and drink.

"He was coming good," Craig states, remembering Connor's last couple of weeks on the firm. "If he'd just given it a bit longer, he could have been good!"

"Nah, he hated working for me," Palmer slurs decisively. "And besides, he'd started something on his own. Don't actually know what that was, but he had something good goin' on, apparently."

"Yeah. I was wonderin' about that," Craig frowns and nods his large head. "You reckon he was doing somethin' for Jennings again? Could be he got back in with some wrong people – kickin' Connor like that, it's the kinda thing Jennings would get one of his 'men' to do."

"Yeah...like that Hickey character," Palmer agrees, tipping back his head to empty his glass yet again. "I'd like to kick that fucker's head in. He's slime."

"Yeah, but thankfully you don't have a likin' for

violence," Craig's frown grows even deeper as he glares at his best friend with concern in his eyes. "So don't get any stupid ideas in that drunk head of yours!"

"But what if he did it?" Palmer asks, his jumbled thoughts falling into some kind of chaotic order. "What if that little shit murdered my brother? Am I supposed to let him get away with it?"

"You want your mother to lose both her sons?" Craig asks with surprising clarity considering the whiskey he's drunk.

"Damn it, Craig! I can't let that little shit walk around scot free," Palmer declares angrily.

"But we don't know that he did it," Craig insists, trying to instil reason into the conversation.

"Yes we do! But I'll hire a PI just to make sure." Palmer sinks down lower into his seat on the settee, his glass falling to the floor.

Standing, none to steadily, Craig lifts Palmer and lays him on his bed. Then he makes himself comfortable at the side of him.

No sense waistin' a comfy lookin' bed!

When Palmer awakes the next morning his head feels like a sledgehammer is still hitting it. He leans forward, head in hands and elbows on his knees, and just sits for endless minutes.

"You still alive?" a deep brown voice grumbles from behind him and makes Palmer jump.

"Jesus! Don't do that!" he cringes, his head throbbing wildly.

"Get the kettle on, boy," Craig orders, while gingerly sitting his large frame upright in the bed.

"You get the kettle on," Palmer counters, not sure he is even capable of standing.

"Your place!"

"Your idea to get drunk!"

"Fuck!" With that pitiful oath, Craig gets to his feet and stretches his considerable bulk to ease out the kinks. Then he pads over to the kettle and switches it on.

The loud rumble of the kettle is enough to have Craig scurrying away to sit on a settee.

"So what's the plan?" he asks Palmer when he finally moves to join him.

"Plan?" he repeats inanely.

"Hickey!" Craig states the single word like it has a world of meaning in it.

"That murdering fucker!"

"That would be the one," Craig confirms with a groan having heard the kettle click off.

"Stay there," Palmer tells him, holding up a staying hand. "I'll make it."

"Good. I don't know that I could have gotten up anyway," Craig admits, rubbing his sore head.

"I don't know what to do about him," Palmer admits, handing the big guy a mug of strong black coffee. "I don't just want the monkey; I want the organ-grinder to go down hard, too!"

"You talkin' about goin' after Jennings?" Craig watches Palmer and sees the intent in his blue eyes harden with remembered rage.

Nodding, Palmer stares into his half-drunk coffee and tries to formulate a plan.

"I think a PI would be a good first step," he reasons out loud. "I need to get as much background information on Jennings and Hickey as possible. I want to know what his other business interests are. What kind of scams he runs and who he runs them with."

"You keep sayin' I, but I think you mean we," Craig prods himself with a thick finger in his considerable chest.

"No, I got it right the first time," Palmer states firmly. "You've got Carly now, you need to take care of her.

"And I will," Craig nods in agreement, "right after we get Jennings and Hickey locked up good and tight!"

"Craig-"

"Do you not know me at all," Craig demands fiercely. "Do you honestly expect me to stand by and watch you get murdered the way Connor was – cause you really don't know me if you think that!"

Getting to his feet, Palmer paces the room then comes to a stop beside his friend.

Holding out his hand to Craig, Palmer smiles, "You and me, we'll fry their hides!"

CHAPTER SEVENTEEN

Alone in her room, Zoe is faced with a hard choice. Does she move back to Birmingham to live with her mother as she'd asked? Or should she go back to Looe and her new life in Cornwall?

I love being back with my mother, but I'm going to be a mother soon, too. Maybe it's time to cut the apron strings, to grow up and move on. But does that have to mean losing touch?

And if I stay it will mean seeing Palmer. It hurts so bad to be near him. I can't help loving him, no matter how hard I try not to. I look at him and remember his touch, my skin burns with it, my lips ache to kiss him.

But I have to stop thinking this way. I need to cut him out of my life. Her hand caresses her stomach, loving her daughter while she is still in her womb. I need to cut him out of our lives! We'll only get hurt all the more if I don't!

"I'll take good care of you, Brook," she whispers to her baby. "Mummy will make sure you have everything you need."

A week later she sits in the same room having dressed all in black to attend Connor's funeral.

The Coroner had deemed Connor's death an unlawful killing, but had released his body for burial after the police had made no complaint.

They had everything they needed to pursue the murderer - as much as Connor could tell them without speaking a single word.

Forensics these days are so astounding. The police have all manner of hidden weapons in their arsenal.

And Zoe could only hope that they would use them well!

Only two of Connor's friends turned up to pay their respects. It was a sad sight, a poor reflection on a young man whose life had been so brutally cut short. But at least they had come.

And then there was Laura. She was so distressed that it was down to Dorothy to offer her comfort. Zoe simply couldn't.

She sat with her mother and Craig. Her eyes never left

the coffin that was sealed at the front of the funeral home.

No one had been allowed to see Connor's face without the bandages. The injuries had been deemed too upsetting for family to see.

I'm glad. I want to remember you the way you were. So handsome, with such a lovely smile and a quirky grin that spelled trouble in a nice way. Though I know you had a troubled side, I'm glad that I got to know another side of you. A loving side that I'm sure I would have grown to love. I was half-way there...we just needed more time...

Unlike Laura, who was sobbing loudly, Zoe didn't cry. She just sat and watched and thought about Connor.

His father and brother both gave moving eulogies, but Zoe didn't hear them.

The day passed in a blur of emotions – a blissful haze that secluded Zoe from all those around her.

Goodbye, Connor. Look in on us sometimes. We'll always remember you!

The bank has forwarded a letter to Palmer, kept by them until the event of Connor Johnson's death at which time it was to be forwarded to his brother, Palmer Johnson, by his own instruction.

Sitting by himself in his huge, lonely loft apartment, Palmer holds it, turning the letter over in his hands, hesitating to read Connor's last communication to him.

Almost reverently, he finally opens the envelope and takes out a couple of sheets of paper with Connor's own handwriting on them.

For endless minutes he reads and rereads Connor's letter, until finally his vision blurs so much that he can't read another word.

Damn it, Connor! Damn it! You could have come to me if you felt like this!

"God damn it!" he yells into the empty room, his hands ready to ball the letter up in his rage, but stopping just short of doing so.

"I'll get the money to her," he says, talking as though Connor was in the room with him. "I'll make sure she's alright."

Moving to the kitchen area of his loft, Palmer pours himself a large whiskey then downs half the glass.

He doesn't want to think about or feel anything for a while. Just blank it all out...just for a while. Jesus Connor...Jesus...

The following morning, Palmer wakes to hear someone thumping at his door.

Christ, stop, just...bloody hell!

Stumbling to the door, Palmer opens it to find Craig looking none too pleased.

"What the fuck...?" Palmer frowns darkly.

"I had a feelin' I'd find you like this," Craig pushes his way past Palmer and gives him one of his meanest glares.

"Get out," Palmer orders without preamble, still holding the door to his flat open.

"You stink!" Craig tells him, not making any move to leave. "And you're still dressed in the clothes you were wearing yesterday, so I can guess you slept in them!"

Slamming the door shut, Palmer has to grab his head to keep it on his shoulders.

"Jesus! What are you doing here? Can't you just leave me in peace, damn it!"

"So you can go back to boozin' and feelin' sorry for yourself?" Craig growls. "I don't think so!"

Walking to his kitchen, Palmer puts the kettle on then turns to glare back at Craig.

"Did Carly send you?" he snaps angrily.

"No! I went into the office and you weren't there. Apparently no one knew when or if you were coming in," Craig tells him, still fixing Palmer with an intense glare.

"Shit! I don't know when I was planning to go into the office or to any of the sites," Palmer replies, his hand pushing back through his blond dishevelled hair. "I don't know anything about anything just now...ok."

"Ordinarily I'd say ok, but this is not how you usually

handle things," Craig tells him having picked up an empty whiskey bottle and a discarded glass.

"Well losing my brother isn't exactly run of the mill," Palmer snaps, then turns to hand Craig a mug of coffee. "He sent me a letter," he tells Craig, his voice softening with the change of subject. "He's dead, and he sent me a letter through his bloody bank to be delivered on the event of his death. What the fuck is that all about!"

"This it?" Craig asks having picked up the crumpled letter from the floor in the sitting area.

He watches Palmer nod then turns his attention back to the letter he's holding. "You want me to read it?"

Palmer nods again, then drinks his overly strong black coffee.

"Christ! No wonder you went under," Craig observes, his head shaking in disbelief. "Did he ever talk to you about this? About feelin' second best, second in every way that counts," he frowns, continuing to read the last words from Connor.

"No. I had no idea he felt like that, and that's what makes me so angry. I could have helped him to realise his own worth," Palmer rubs a hand over his tired, weary eyes. "My parents were always comparing us. Always holding me up as the success story he had to try to match. I knew he resented that – damn it, I would have if I were him. But he never said it went deeper than that, nothing like what he's said in there," Palmer says, nodding towards the letter Craig is still holding.

"I gather you're not planning to show this to your mother?" Craig looks at his haggard looking friend and feels nothing but pity now.

Shaking his head, Palmer takes the letter Craig is holding out to him and carefully folds the crumpled sheets of paper.

"It would kill my mother to know that this is how Connor felt. That he bounced his way from one mess to another because he never felt good enough," he tells his friend, then sits heavily onto a settee. "And I feel bad for not realising, for thinking of Connor as just a pain in my rear end. I should have known there was something deeper at the back of it all!"

"You ever find out where to get those omniscient powers you don't forget to tell me," Craig chuckles deeply. "Hindsight is always 20:20, you can't carry on beating yourself up like this. For one, Zoe is goin' to need some support. And I know you know I don't mean the financial sort."

Again, Palmer nods and considers his friend's words. "It looks like Connor's got that covered – though how the hell he ever managed to make so much money in such a short space of time is anyone's guess."

Now it's Craig's turn to sit and nod. "I've been thinkin' about that. As Connor's executor, you can get hold of his bank details – you know, statements and the like. Well maybe, you could try and work out where the money came from?"

"Damn! I didn't even think of that!" Palmer admits, his head finally starting to clear.

"It's hard to think through a bottle of whiskey," Craig chuckles knowingly. "I've tried, it doesn't work. And in the end, it doesn't help either."

"Stop fretting, I'm not going to make a habit of it! But it was hard – seeing Zoe like that, all cut up over my brother... I think the baby's mine, Craig," he tells his friend, who doesn't look too surprised by the statement.

"I agree," Craig is nodding thoughtfully. "I've thought about it a lot, what with bein' with her mother en'all. It's the only thing that makes any sense. Problem is, you can't prove it unless Zoe cooperates, and she doesn't want a bar of you right now."

"Could you talk to her?" Palmer asks. "I mean, as you're there most of the time these days, could you just casually ask a few questions?"

Frowning, Craig considers the request. "If I do, it will have to be subtle and not so as it looks like I'm on your side in this," Craig muses out loud. "If Zoe thinks I'm just fishin' on your behalf she'll clam up good and tight. So it might take a while to find out what you want."

"We don't have too long," Palmer reminds him. "Zoe lives in Cornwall now, she has a whole other life there with friends and everything."

"Shit! I forgot about that," Craig admits. "But I still can't go bulldozing my way in, then you won't find out anythin' at all!"

"Just do your best. We need to know when she met up with Connor, how they became a couple and how he was making money hand over fist!"

Again, the big man nods in agreement. "There's no sayin' that Zoe even knows much about that. Connor could be a conniving little so-n-so, he may not have let that slip."

"Then we'll just have to hope that he did, and that his bank statements will show us a money trail that we can follow back to whoever or whatever he was into," Palmer declares, his heart lifting as his determination kicks in.

"We're going to find out who did this to Connor – who beat him so badly that his own mother wasn't allowed to see his face before they buried him," Palmer states, getting up to release some pent up energy.

"Damn straight!" Craig agrees. "And maybe we'll solve

your other mystery – the one with the letters," Craig reminds him. "You still don't know who had it in for you in the first place. Could be this whole thing is connected."

"Damn! Damn! Damn!" Palmer exclaims loudly. "My head is being pulled in so many different directions – how the hell am I supposed to solve this and run a business that is in serious trouble?"

"You've got good people workin' for you – you let them do their jobs while you focus on your private life. It's time to sort this mess out and move on – otherwise it'll hang over you like a goddamned curse!"

"Ok. Ok," Palmer stops his pacing and comes to stand by Craig. "You take the wheel for a while. You run the company and keep things moving while I get this mess sorted. Deal?" And he holds his hand out to his best friend.

"Shit!" Craig frowns uncertainly, then takes his friend's hand and shakes it firmly. "Deal!"

CHAPTER EIGHTEEN

"I'm ok, mum," Zoe tries hard to placate her fretful mother. "I have a little cottage and a good job that I love. And I'm going to the doctor for regular check-ups on the baby," she explains when her mother still looks doubtful.

"But a mother should be with her daughter at a time like this," Carly reasons. "How can I help you, support you, when you insist on living at the other end of the country?"

Racking her brains for something to say that will make her choice make sense, Zoe eventually gives up.

"Mum, this is just something I need to do. I'll stay for a week, or so, but then I need to get back. It isn't fair on Tara to stay away any longer than that," she pleads.

Carly decides to accept what she can for now, and nods in agreement. "Ok, I'll just have to take some emergency leave. It's not like I've ever done it before," she reasons, hoping her boss will see it that way.

"Mum, no. I won't have you putting your job at risk. We can see each other in the evenings and over the weekend," Zoe tells her. "And you have Craig now," she adds with a smile. "I'm really happy for you."

Carly feels her cheeks heat and only hopes that she isn't blushing. "Craig is not the point," she tells Zoe firmly. "You come first, he already knows that."

Laughing, Zoe shakes her head. "Oh no you don't, you're not using me to pull back from Craig!"

"What...I was not!" Carly denies, then has to wonder if Zoe is right. Things have been going so well with Craig that it has become a little frightening. "Well...not deliberately," she concedes, then rolls her eyes at Zoe's laugh.

"I like him," Carly continues. "There, I said it...I really like him. And, yes, it is a little scary."

"I do understand, you know. After all these years on your own, and after what dad did, you're bound to be a little nervous," Zoe smiles.

"Well hark at the agony aunt talk," Carly again rolls her eyes. "But you're right. I suppose those are valid reasons for my being careful," she states, being a little more select in her terminology.

"Ok, well, don't get overly 'careful' and end up losing a really lovely man," Zoe advises more seriously. "You've been on your own long enough, mum; it doesn't have to be that way anymore."

"Ok. Ok. But back to you and me - you will keep in touch, and not through your dad?" Carly asks, finally realising that she isn't going to be able to talk Zoe into staying.

"No. I'll call and write and you can call and write to me," Zoe tells her, then watches her mums eyes fill with glistening tears. "Don't do that. I hate when you cry!"

"I'm not crying," Carly swipes her eyes defiantly. "I'm just so happy to have you back in my life. I hated losing you that way. I was so lost without you, and so worried about what you were going through all alone."

"I'm ok, mum. I really am," Zoe assures her. "I'm unbelievably sad inside about Connor, but I know I'll be ok. I just need some time to sort myself out."

"Did you love him?" Carly asks, not sure how far to push for information, but wanting to know if her daughter's heart has been broken for a second time.

"Not in the same way that I love Palmer, no," Zoe admits quietly. "But I cared for him deeply. He was just so kind and supportive, a completely different person to the one I thought I knew when I lived here."

"So...you still love Palmer?"

It is Zoe's turn to have her eyes fill with unshed tears, and her mother reaches over to take her hand. "It's ok, sweetheart. I know how hard you fell for Palmer, and how much you were looking forward to marrying him. That's why it was such a shock when you left, I knew it would take something pretty bad to drive you away."

Nodding, Zoe tries to swallow the lump in her throat and head off the crying jag that is threatening. "That bouquet of red roses that was delivered to the suite we were all in had a letter attached, like the ones I had been getting - like the one I got delivered here," Zoe reminds her mother. "Only this one had a couple of photos in with it. They show Palmer kissing another woman, though he still denies ever being unfaithful to me. I just don't get how he can do that?"

"Have you shown him the photos, confronted him with the evidence?"

"No. And I was in such a state over Connor that I didn't think to bring them with me."

Carly hesitates, then takes a deep breath and plunges into deep emotional waters where her daughter is concerned. She has always tried not to pry, but there is something she just needs to know. "Is the baby Palmer's?"

A single tear escapes Zoe's eyes as she nods and bites down on her bottom lip. Then she says, "I didn't find out until I was already living in the cottage that dad bought me. It was a total shock but I never doubted that I wanted to keep it. She's mine, as I was yours," Zoe's watery smile confirms.

Reaching her hand up to cup her daughter's cheek, Carly nods with understanding. "You'll be a fine mother. You have a large heart and a good brain. You'll figure out what's best for the two of you. And, if that's Palmer, then so be it."

"You'd approve if I got back with him? But what about the letters – the photos?" Zoe asks, dumbfounded.

Pursing her lips and shaking her head, Carly tells her, "I don't believe we know all there is to know about that, not yet. I'm not saying that Palmer is completely innocent – maybe he is, or maybe he isn't – but it does strike me as odd that they waited until your wedding day to deliver the photos," Carly observes. "It's like, stopping the wedding was the ultimate goal. And let's face it, if they had sent them before the wedding day it would have given you time to show Palmer and him time to prove his innocence. But as it was, you did the only thing those photos were intent on making you do, you left without saying a word. Palmer didn't get the chance to clear his name and the wedding was cancelled – can you think of anyone who would have wanted that?"

Zoe's head is shaking, her brows furrowed as her mind goes deep in thought.

"I never thought of it like that," she admits, confused by the idea of someone carrying out such a devious plot. "But I don't have any idea who would have wanted that. Except..." *No! That's ridiculous! I'll never believe that!*

"You have an idea...?" Carly pushes gently.

"No. No, it's just a silly thought that popped into my head. It's nothing," she insists, her lips pursing tight against voicing such a stupid idea.

Knowing when not to push her daughter, Carly nods and changes the subject. "Laura looked devastated at the funeral. Was she very in love with Connor?"

Glad of the change of subject, Zoe nods fervently. "Unfortunately, yes. Apparently Connor had tried to break things off a few times, but he said that Laura just wouldn't take no for an answer and clung tighter than a limpet." Then Zoe winces at the poor turn of phrase. "He said she just wouldn't let go, so he left."

"Is that how you met up?" Carly frowns.

"No. At least, I don't think so," Zoe shakes her head. "We met by accident – Connor had rented a beautiful house in Millendreath, just up the coast from Looe where my cottage is. I just walked out of the florist shop where I work and all but walked into him – it was such a shock, I can tell you," Zoe laughs, still amazed at the coincidence of it all.

"And he was there on holiday – or business?" Carly asks curiously.

"Oh, holiday," Zoe confirms quickly. "The house he rented was beautiful. It had a swimming pool and terrific sea views. And he let me use the pool whenever I wanted. He was so different, once I got to know him. Not at all like he was when we were here."

"And, you just fell for him," Carly suggests tentatively.

"No, not really. It was more of a gradual thing. Connor was so supportive," she smiles at her mother, the memories such happy ones. "I knew he'd always liked me – well, maybe more than that," she admits, her cheeks burning at the memory. "And I didn't realise how lonely I'd been. It was just so easy with Connor – he really wanted to take care of us; me and the baby. You should have seen his face when we found out it was a girl, he was over the moon and immediately chose the name Brook – so that's what she will be named," Zoe finishes softly, her memories becoming difficult to relive.

"Brook Johnson, that's a lovely name," Carly smiles happily.

"Yes it is. And he was so looking forward to being a daddy – he was really going to look after us," she repeats, wanting her mother to understand just how much Connor had been willing to take on.

"So, you think perhaps he loved you?"

Nodding, Zoe can't hold back the tears any longer. "He did. He really did. And now he's gone before he could ever meet Brook. It's so wrong and so sad. I don't understand who would hurt him like that. They deserve to die!" she states, all her pent up pain flooding out along with a deluge of tears.

Pulling her daughter into her arms, Carly rocks her and strokes her hair like she did when Zoe was a little girl.

"I know Palmer is trying to find out what happened," Carly whispers softly. "Craig told me they have been going over a lot of things, trying to back track and find out who might have been holding a grudge."

"Then I hope they give whoever it is a taste of their own medicine," Zoe declares uncharacteristically. "They deserve to suffer the way Connor did, and then they should be locked up for the rest of their lives!"

Deciding not to reproach Zoe's vengeful thoughts, Carly merely holds her daughter and tries to sooth the hurt that is tearing her heart in two.

"They'll do what needs to be done," Carly assures her.

"Craig is adamant that the two of them will find out who was behind it all."

Palmer has taken all of the paperwork home that pertains to Connor, his employment with his company and anything else he deems relevant.

He's bought an easel and a large white board and a pack of coloured dry wipe pens. Now he's half way through drawing a mind map — something used to organise thoughts centred around a certain issue. In this case, the issue is Connor and his name sits at the centre.

Palmer has drawn a circle around Connor's name, then drawn lines out from it and labelled them with different ideas. Like, Jennings, Hickey, Laura, Zoe, and so on. Then he's made a timeline that runs along the bottom of the board.

It covers things like Connor joining his company. Some of the significant jobs he worked on. The timing of his involvement with Jennings, the beating and the payoff of his debt. Stuff like that — but so far Palmer has been unable to connect any of the dots.

Craig'll be here soon. Maybe he'll think of something to add that'll make more sense. So far it's just names and dates, nothing to suggest when things changed or went wrong for Connor.

Just then the doorbell rings and Palmer moves to open the door.

"Hey, how're you doin'," Craig asks in his usual gravelly voice.

"I think I'm making some progress, but I have no idea where it's leading me," Palmer confesses.

Craig moves across the room to see what Palmer has been working on and stands nodding then frowning at the whiteboard.

"What about the letters?" he asks bluntly.

"What...?"

"The letters," Craig repeats. "You haven't got them on you board, not even on the timeline," he states, his large finger pointing to the lack of any notation. "If you're goin' to do this you need all the facts, not just a select few."

Nodding, Palmer picks up a pen and begins to write. "I'll put L for letters and just a brief bit about where they were left or delivered," he suggests, and continues to mark the timeline with the relevant information.

"There, that should do it," he tells Craig, taking a step back to look at his larger than life friend for approval.

"Yep, that's better. Now, what about the date you met Zoe, when it got serious and any incidents that might have happened in between times?" Craig suggests.

"You really think that's necessary?" Palmer frowns, but moves to do as the big guy suggested.

Then his frown goes deeper, his eyes narrowing as he

looks at the timeline. "Actually, there's another item that should go about here," Palmer says, then begins writing on the board.

"He did what?!" Craig growls, his eyes growing hot with anger.

"Connor assaulted Zoe in the company car park after she locked up one night," Palmer confirms, having noted the incident on the board.

"Jesus! If that boy wasn't already dead I'd be kicking his arse ten shades of black and blue for doing that," Craig states angrily.

"Well someone beat you to it...," Palmer grimaces, "...that's why we're doing this, remember?"

"Jesus!" Craig has a hard time reining his temper in, but knows that his friend is right. "Ok. Fuck it! I can't look at that for now," Craig growls, and takes himself off to the seating area of Palmer's loft flat. "Don't you have anythin' else I can be lookin' at?"

"As a matter of fact...," Palmer walks over to a manila file on his kitchen work-top and takes it over to Craig, "...you can browse through these. I did like you said, I contacted the bank, told them what I was doing and asked for the last twelve months bank statements for Connor's bank account."

"Good. This is good," Craig nods, leafing through the

list of incomings and outgoings. "You know, a beer might aid my concentration," he lifts a brow to Palmer and gets a smiling nod in reply.

Going off to the fridge, Palmer takes out two cans of beer and hands one to Craig. "Here you go, big guy. You see anything obvious?"

Raising his eyes up to look at Palmer, Craig gives him an impressive glare. "Get back to your damned board and leave this to me!"

CHAPTER NINETEEN

A second later and Palmer is back from the board and standing over Craig.

"Christ almighty, that boy was into somethin' big. He's got a sudden rush of huge deposits goin' into his account, and he's spendin' like he hasn't got but a minute to live. Here..." and he hands Palmer one of Connor's bank statements, "...you see, that's where it starts but it continues right up to the day he died. He must have made whatever kind of transaction it was during his time back here and got himself beaten half to death shortly after!"

"Knowing Connor, he pissed someone off big time!" Palmer walks back to his white board and begins jotting down the payments on the timeline. "Here, take a look at this," Palmer beckons over his friend. "There's something here that I can't see – I can feel it but I can't see it."

Craig hauls himself to his feet, taking the bank statements with him.

Perusing all the information, Craig agrees. "I know what you're sayin' but I don't see it yet either. But we will," he states positively. "We will!"

Going back to his seat, Craig continues to look for patterns in the cash-flow. Then he spots something significant. "You ever hear of The Hamblin' Agency?" he asks Palmer, and receives a shake of his head in reply. "Well I have...," he states, holding the bank statement out for Palmer to read it, "...we were thinkin' about hiring a PI to find Zoe and this is one I looked at."

Palmer frowns down at the outgoing payment to the private investigation company and then looks at Craig. "So, what would Connor need a PI for? Do you think it was to do with this business thing he had going on?"

Shaking his head, Craig says, "Look at the date – the timing is too exact to be a fluke."

"Christ!" Palmer pushes his hands back through his blond hair and lets out a gust of breathe. "Right after the wedding! Do you think he hired them to find Zoe?"

"Oh yeah," Craig growls deep in his throat. "I think Connor went after her the minute you were off the scene. After what you say he did in the car park, it would make perfect sense!"

With a mighty yell, Palmer throws his half-full beer bottle across the room and it smashes loudly into the kitchen cupboards. "Just when I'm trying to see another side to him we find something like this! What the fuck! What the fuck was he doing trying to find Zoe?!"

I need to talk to Zoe, find out when and how they met up. If I'm reading this right, Connor always wanted her; the car park incident was just his first outward exhibition of it. But what if he was determined to have her, what would he have done to make that happen?

"I'm going to need your help," he tells Craig. "I have to talk to Zoe and find out what's been going on. If I ask her over to dinner will you just suggest to Carly that it might be a good idea for us to straighten things out?"

"You mean, clear the way as it were," Craig frowns, then nods his approval. "Sounds like you two need to talk, straighten out some of these misunderstandin's and the like!"

"Ok. That's great. I'll be over tomorrow at about 8 o'clock just to visit; I'll make up some excuse, like the money that Carter has left to Zoe. We'll talk, then I'll ask her to come over for dinner and we'll see where we go from there," Palmer suggests, all the while pacing like a nervous suitor.

"Just remember...," Craig's dark brown voice rumbles

out slowly, "...you won the lady's heart once, take your time and tread carefully, and you can do it again."

Jennings is livid. In his large, plush, backroom office, he is pacing around like a caged tiger who wants to rip someone's throat out.

The he looks at the screen that shows him what is going on outside in his bar and sees Hickey walk in with a cocky grin.

Pressing the button near the screen, he waits for one of his lackeys to bring Hickey to him, as arranged.

He moves to sit behind his desk and calms his raging pulse and puts on a poker face.

As his office door opens, he can hear Hickey protesting at being shown through the back like just another patsy. He doesn't know his job description has changed from 'Chief Hood and Head Cracker' to 'Pain in the Arse Floor Cleaner'!

"Hey, hey, watch the suit," he protests when one of the escort party gives his arm a shove. "Hey, Mr Jennings, tell these apes to lay off. What's going on here?"

Looking at the piece of shit that has just been brought into his office, Jennings leans back in his seat and simply stares.

Tempeling his fingers, he moves the tip to his mouth contemplatively, then smiles. It is a slow, feline smile that makes Hickey's blood run cold.

He's seen that smile before. He's watched the people on the other end of it cack themselves at the thought of what is coming next.

"Mr Jennings, sir..." he begins, "...I think..." But Jennings tuts and shakes his head.

"You see, that's the problem," Jennings tells him so quietly that Hickey has to listen hard to hear him. "I've been trying to work out what the problem was, and now you have solved it. Right there, that's the problem."

Moving to sit a little more upright, Jennings' large leather chair rocks slowly forward. "When did I start paying you to think?"

Hickey looks taken aback, the hairs on the back of his neck standing to attention and a bead of sweat trickles slowly down his jellified spine.

"I.I just thought...I mean..."

"Again with the thinking," Jennings shakes his head, purses his lips and frowns over his impressive desk to the dead man sitting on the other side. "I pay you to inflict a few bruises, maybe break a few bones, or even permanently remove the vermin from my life — but the one thing I don't pay you for, is to think," and Jennings wags a finger at Hickey like he's been a naughty boy.

"No, sir. No thinking," he agrees nervously.

"No, no thinking," Jennings repeats, his eyes

narrowing in on his target. "You weren't thinking when you went after Connor Johnson, were you?" he asks, though Hickey knows he doesn't expect an answer. He's seen this routine before, too. "And you weren't thinking when you beat that little shit to within an inch of his pathetic life, were you?" His voice has gradually gone even quieter so that, now, Hickey is having to lean forward to hear him.

"You left a trail right to my door," Jennings states, his cheeks beginning to redden with the effort of maintaining his tight control. "Now I'm going to have to deal with his wealthy brother. You know, the one with all the smarts that his little brother didn't have!" And he watches the light go on in Hickey's dumbass brain. "That's right. Palmer Johnson, 'the big man' as Connor Johnson used to call him. That's right, isn't it?" he asks Hickey, like they're pals again. "That is what you told me, right?"

"Right...," Hickey smiles, beginning to relax just a little, "...he did! That's right! He couldn't stand the guy."

"Yet 'the big man' came in here and stumped up a hundred grand to bail his 'pain in the arse' brother out," Jennings states, lifting a brow.

Hickey actually laughs, looks across the desk to his executioner and laughs. "H.he hated that," he tells his boss with a sneering grin. "I heard it from his drinking buddies, he really hated that his brother bailed him out."

"So...and I'm giving you permission now to engage your brain...why do you think he did that?" Jennings asks, quietly, reasonably, angrily.

"Who, Connor...?" But Hickey watches Jennings shake a finger at him and tries again. "Oh, you mean Palmer – why did he bail his brother out?" And he watches his boss nod silently. "Cause he's a big assed jerk," Hickey laughs again. "Least ways, that's what Connor told his pals."

Now Jennings sits very still, only the pulse jumping in his neck gives anything away.

The colour drains from his face as he contemplates the vermin sat in front of him.

The more his boss stares at him, the more hesitant Hickey's laughter becomes. Until, finally, it chokes him and he has to cough to take his next breath.

"Now the big assed jerk is going to be looking for baby brother's killer," Jennings whispers, his eyes boring into Hickey's. "And you work for me, so that brings him to my door."

"No. No. I'll take care of him," Hickey offers when he sees where the conversation just turned. "I won't let him get near you," he states bravely.

"But you're the one who put that fucker on my tail," Jennings states, his voice beginning to get just a little louder. "You had to think, had to take matters into your own hands," he tells Hickey, the colour in his cheeks now turning an unhealthy shade of purple.

"Why? Did he call you a few unpleasant names? Or was it because he took his flashy car back," Jennings asks, remembering how much Hickey had loved his short lived status symbol.

"No. No sir," Hickey shakes his head fiercely. "He put a contract out on me. He paid a few cokeheads I know to whack me," he states, sounding outraged by the audacity of the plan. "But what he didn't realise is, they're loyal to me," and he jabs a finger into his puffed up chest. "They came to me the minute he left. I let them keep the money he paid them as they'd done me a good turn. But I told them, they'd be helping me take Johnson out instead," and again, he laughs at his own cunning.

A smile actually graces Jennings' lips as he nods in understanding. "I see. I get it. He had the cheek to hire your own thugs to take you out so, of course, the slimeball had to be wiped out." And Jennings watches Hickey nod rapidly again.

"Yeah, that's it. The little shit!"

Getting to his feet, Jennings stays on his side of the desk, not trusting himself to get any nearer to Hickey as he begins to pace back and forth, his hands clasped behind his back.

"So, the slime-ball hurt your feelings. He dented your pride. And for this, for daring to pay a few coke-heads to whack you, you beat the living crap out of him!" Jennings muses, almost to himself. Then he stops pacing and turns to glare at Hickey. "And that's when you made your biggest mistake. You started thinking," he states angrily, his eyes beginning to bulge in his round head. "Instead of coming to me, instead of letting me do the thinking, you tried engaging what little brain you have in that thick head and came up with a fucked up plan to bring Palmer Johnson knocking at my door!"

"No sir! I would never let that happen," Hickey tells him, then notices the two goons who had escorted him to his boss' office move a little closer. "No. I can take care of this. I can set things right," he pleads, sudden dawning now freezing the blood in his veins.

"Yes...," Jennings agrees, "...you can. By dying," he grins, then gives the two goons a nod that brings them to Hickey's side.

"Gag him, then take him out and kick the crap out of him till he looks like Connor Johnson did when this fucking idiot finished with him. Then dump his dead arse outside Palmer Johnson's builder's yard – payment made. Score settled!" Jennings smiles as Hickey fights to free himself, knowing his fate is sealed.

But even when his office is calm again, Jennings' temper still takes time to settle. He's never been implicated in any crime. He paid the likes of Hickey to bloody their own hands and take the mess away from his door.

But now you've led them right to me. So let's just wait and see what Palmer's next move will be. Maybe Hickey's death will be enough to appease 'the big man', or maybe not.

But if he comes sniffing too close to my door...well...I'll just have to arrange a reunion with his brother after all!

CHAPTER TWENTY

Sitting in her mother's garden, Zoe is reading a book and trying hard to get over the loss of Connor.

She has always found reading to be totally absorbing, able to immerse herself fully into the story.

But today she is struggling, because not only is she trying to put Connor and any possible future with him firmly in the past, she now needs to stop thinking about Palmer too.

What good does loving him do? She asks herself as she finally lays the open book on her knees. I can't have him. I can't trust him. So why am I always thinking about him?

Her body has betrayed her many times. She has woken in the night with such a burning need for Palmer that she has had to scratch that particularly insistent itch herself.

And then she has spent the rest of the night dreaming of his hands on her, his mouth on hers, his cock moving inside of her.

Jesus, woman! You're a masochist thinking like this! All you're doing is torturing yourself with something, someone, you can never have. Ever, if you know what's good for you!

"Zoe?" Palmer's voice at the back gate makes her start so violently that Zoe's drink goes all over her and she has to shake the book out quickly to rid it of orange juice.

"Palmer, is that you?"

"Yeah, I went to the front door but you obviously couldn't hear the bell from out here," his disembodied voice tells her. "Are you going to let me in?"

"Just a minute," she shouts across the back garden, then tries to calm her nerves as she crosses to let the man of her daydreams in.

"What happened?" he asks, eyeing her drink spattered top.

Loath to tell him that he had made her jump, Zoe just says, "A bee. A big bumble bee made me jump and my drink went everywhere."

"Ok," he smiles, not believing a word of it. "You'd

better change that," he tells her, pointing to her top and the fact that her bare breasts are now visible through the almost transparent wet material.

"Oh!" she gasps, clutching a hand over her breast. "Sorry. I won't be a minute." And she dashes indoors to wash off the sticky orange juice and make herself decent.

"Don't mind me," he tells her as he follows slowly in her wake, "the view was lovely from where I'm standing."

In the bathroom, Zoe strips off her top and uses a sponge to freshen up. Then she turns when she hears Palmer at the door.

She hadn't closed it properly and he'd nudged it further open.

"Palmer, you can't be here," she tells him.

"You've never been shy around me before," he tells her, his eyes looking deep into hers until they fall to the heavier swell of her breasts. "Pregnancy suits you. You have a lovely glow and your body is stunning."

"Palmer...I..." Swallowing hard, Zoe tries to calm her breathing. Her pulse just hit double time and her mouth isn't the only place salivating over this man.

Before her brain can form a protest she is in his arms and his hands are doing everything she's been dreaming of. When her head falls back his lips taste a trail down to the jumping pulse in her throat and has it jumping even more erratically.

"Palmer..."

He loves the sound of his name when she breathes it out in that sexy way.

When he dips his head to taste her pregnancy swollen breasts, she bucks in his arms and he has to hold her firmly.

Oh God! I want this man! God help me, I want him so bad!

Carrying her to the bedroom, Palmer removes the rest of her clothing while all the time pleasuring her body, and her responses drive him wild.

You're mine. My wife in spirit if not in law. We belong together. We will be together, now and always, I swear it!

His lips trail down her body, kissing the belly that is keeping their child safe and warm, then moving down to the heat of her womanhood.

Mine!

His mouth devours her, tasting his woman and breathing in her scent.

Mine! Only mine!

Her head is turning side to side on the pillow, her mind lost to sensation and all rational thought pushed away.

When his fingers enter her she screams out, "Yes! Oh god, yes!" And he pleasures her more and more until the waves of her first orgasm shudder through her body.

When he rears up over her, Zoe can only look at him with starved admiration. He is magnificent in his need for her and she needs him just as badly.

Taking him in her hand she pleasures him for just a moment before guiding him inside her.

Her breath catches, her body welcoming the familiarity of him, and her mind explodes with possibilities.

I love you! Oh hell, I love you so much!

"Stay with me, Zoe," he tells her, pumping into her with long drawn out strokes. "Stay with me and let me love you."

I want to say yes. I want to. But...

Sensing her uncertainty, seeing the doubt in her eyes, Palmer pushes himself hard into her asserting his claim.

"You're mine!" he growls, hips pistoning him into her, driving Zoe crazy. "You'll always be mine"

Harder. Faster. Deeper.

On a loud scream, at the peak of her climax and as her mind loses all reason, Zoe finally tells him, "I love you. I love you. I love you."

But as her body recovers and her mind regains reason, she whispers, "But I can't stay with you."

Rolling them on to their sides, still joined so

intimately, Palmer can only hold her in his arms and pray that he can convince her differently.

Stroking her long soft hair, Palmer knows that to push his point now will only push Zoe further away. For now, he will just love her.

"I'll convince you one day," he murmurs against her ear. "I'm working on a lot of things right now, and with Craig's help I'm going to find out what or who is at the back of all my bad luck. Including why I lost you," he tells her, placing a kiss against her hair and realising that she has already fallen asleep.

Stretching and yawning, Zoe wakes a couple of hours later feeling refreshed and... "Oh my god! It really happened! It wasn't a dream," she gasps, her body throbbing in places it had no business to throb in.

"What the hell were you thinking?!" she demands of her reflection in the long dress mirror that stands in the corner of her bedroom.

Getting in the shower seems like the only way to pull herself together and straighten this whole mess out.

And it certainly makes her feel better, if not completely fine with what just happened.

I need to leave! That cannot be allowed to happen again!

Moving around her room, Zoe starts to pack her bag

then stops when she hears a gasp from her open bedroom door.

Her mother looks heartbroken, her eyes focused on the suitcase Zoe is packing. "You're leaving! You were just going to leave without saying goodbye?!"

"Yes...no...I can't stay," Zoe tells her, slumping down heavily on the end of her bed. "I can't handle how I still feel about Palmer. I need to leave," she pleads, elbow on her knee and her forehead resting in her hand.

"You mean you're running away again," Carly accuses, surprising Zoe into sitting upright.

"How can you say that? You know what I've been through, what Palmer did?!"

"I know what someone accused him of," Carly states, unconvinced. "But you've never given him the chance to defend himself, to refute whatever evidence you think you have."

Standing now, hands on hips and feeling let down by her mother's lack of support, Zoe lifts her head defiantly. "I have the photos! I've seen for myself what Palmer is capable of!"

"Then you have nothing to fear by staying," Carly challenges just as defiantly. "If you believe you have all the answers already then nothing Palmer can say will make any difference. But if you have doubts, don't you owe it to yourself...and your child, to make absolutely sure that her father is as guilty as you think he is?"

"Her...I never said that Palmer was her father," Zoe states hesitantly.

"You didn't have to. I know my daughter better than to believe that you slept with someone else right before your wedding," Carly states firmly. "And, if Palmer is half the man I believe he is, he knows it too!"

"Oh lord!" With her knees buckling beneath her, Zoe slumps back down on the bed. "That's not good! That's not good at all! Now he'll want custody...he'll try to take her away from me..."

Watching her daughter's growing hysteria, Carly crosses the room to sit beside her on the bed and puts an arm across her shoulders.

"Even if Palmer were stupid enough to try it, do you think we would ever let that happen?"

"But the courts, they might see my relationship with Connor as grounds to find me an unfit mother?"

"Oh, sweetheart," Carly gathers her daughter to her and gives her a much needed hug, "it doesn't work like that. You already have a good home. And you don't need to work, from what you've told me about the help your father is giving you. So why would the courts take Brook away from you?"

"I don't know," Zoe admits. "It's just, he's so rich and I was frightened that he could buy the best legal experts who would make me look bad. I mean, I have been living with his brother."

"Hmm," Carly sighs deeply. "So, what about Connor – did you love him?"

Rubbing her aching eyes, Zoe turns to her mother and admits, "No. Not in the same way that I have always loved Palmer. But I cared deeply for him, and he knew how I felt. I never lied to Connor."

Nodding, Carly frowns at her own thoughts. "But he was willing to be Brook's father anyway?"

Smiling broadly, Zoe recalls Connor's excitement over the prospect of becoming a daddy. "He wanted to take care of us both," she asserts firmly. "You should have seen his face when we went for the ultrasound. I was worried that he would only care for the baby if it was a boy, but he was thrilled when they told us it was a girl," she laughs at the vivid memory.

"And he chose the name?" Carly smiles.

"He did. Once he'd convinced me to find out the sex of the baby, we started bandying names about, just trying them on for size for a while. But when he found out she was a girl, he stuck with Brook and seemed overjoyed with her."

"Then I'm glad you had what little time you had together. But you can't keep running away. You need to face this thing with Palmer – face it and put it to rest for good!"

CHAPTER TWENTY-ONE

The police are already on scene when Palmer arrives at work. The badly beaten body of a man has been discovered on his property.

Laura had been the one to find him and had called the police in hysterics on her mobile. Scared witless she sits waiting in a police car, with a female officer, for one of the detectives to take her statement.

Before he can speak to anyone or enter the building, Palmer is put into a police car and taken to the station for questioning.

"A bit of a coincidence, isn't it, that your brother gets himself beaten half to death and then another body turns up beaten in an identical fashion?" the inspector asks Palmer for the umpteenth time.

"I keep telling you, I don't know anything about the body. I didn't even know there was a body until I arrived at my office," Palmer states, keeping his calm with great effort. "Now, I am answering your questions voluntarily, and without a solicitor present, but if you're going to start accusing me of beating someone to death then that is going to change!"

The inspector eyes him, glances up at his colleague and then back to Palmer. "According to the ID in a wallet found on the body, the man's name was David Hickey." Then seeing a flash of recognition on Palmer's face, the inspector says, "I see you know the name. Did you know the man?" he asks, moving his face just a little nearer to Palmer's over the desk between them.

"I knew Hickey," Palmer confesses. "Or I should say, I had the miserable pleasure of meeting him a couple of times."

"So...," the inspector nods, "...not exactly a fan."

"He was a heavy, working for a local hood who my brother owed a lot of money to," Palmer tells them frankly. "I had to meet up with Hickey to pay him the money otherwise Connor was going to die."

Silently, the inspector nods and sits back in his seat. "So you already knew the guy had it in for your brother — who's to say he didn't follow through even though you paid him off? Then you might have followed through seeing as how your brother turned up beat to shit!"

"Ok, that's it!" Getting to his feet, Palmer looks from one inspector to the other, "You either charge me or I'm walking out of here."

He sees the men exchange looks and then the seated one gives the other a nod to open the door. But just before Palmer can walk through it he asks, "So what's the name of this hood you were talking about?"

"Jennings. He isn't hard to find," Palmer says then turns and strides away, leaving them to work it out for themselves.

Stepping out of the police station, Palmer takes out his mobile and calls Craig.

"We need to meet. Can you make 9 o'clock at my place? Yep, it's a shitty start to the day alright. I just got out of the police station – we'll talk back at my place," he tells a very worried Craig. "Ok. Bye."

Looking around him, Palmer watches people bustling by, getting on with their lives like nothing has happened. And, of course, for them it hasn't – but his life has just become very sticky and very complicated.

Not only has his brother been murdered, but the man who was most likely responsible for Connor's death had himself been killed.

Getting himself dumped on Palmer's business premises automatically shone the spotlight right on the man himself. And, due to his brother's murder, he had motive.

Not that the police were aware of the connection yet. At least, not fully.

But it wouldn't take them long, not now that he had given them Jennings' name.

But what else could he do? Jennings was almost certainly hip deep in this mess!

Yes, you little ratfink, I'll bet you took Hickey out then left him on my doorstep as some sort of payback!

Well...I'm coming, Jennings, you can count on that!

After stopping off to sort out a few errands, Palmer arrives back at his flat to find Craig leaning against his car waiting for him.

"Sorry, I didn't have any food, had to make a quick stop off," Palmer tells him, heaving a couple of heavy carrier bags out of the boot of his car.

The loft feels exquisitely cool after the unusually hot morning they'd been treated to.

Putting the carrier bags on the dining table, Palmer begins to unpack them.

"The police think I had something to do with Hickey's murder," Palmer tells Craig, getting right to the point. "I suppose I can understand that, given that he's almost certainly the one who killed Connor – but they're not fully aware of all that. Yet...," he adds ominously.

"What did you tell them?" Craig draws out a chair and sits his large frame down at the dining table and watches Palmer continue to unpack his groceries.

"Everything. Connor's debt, the payoff; I even gave them Jennings' name." Turning to screw up the now empty carrier bags and dump them in the bin, Palmer eyes his friend uncertainly. "You think I shouldn't have?"

Pursing his lips, Craig considers for a moment. "I think Jennings is at the back of this no matter how you look at it. But I've been wonderin' about the dump – if he was just lookin' at pointin' a finger at you, why make such an obvious move? I mean, if you had taken Hickey out in revenge for your brother's death, would you really dump his body in your own back yard, so to speak?"

"So, you don't think this was about making me look guilty of Hickey's murder?"

Palmer draws out a dining chair and joins his friend in sitting at the table.

"I think Jennings' made you a gift," Craig says, surprising the hell out of Palmer.

"A gift! What the fuck?!"

Craig nods his large head while eyeing Palmer, who

looks shocked by his suggestion. "Yep, that's what I think. I also think Hickey did your brother off his own back – it just don't make sense for Jennings to order Connor dead. He had his money, and like you said at the time, it was just business...and you took care of that. So why would he order Connor beaten to death?" Again, the big man purses his lips and shakes his head.

"So you think Jennings took care of a little housekeeping problem then offered him up as some sort of settlement?" Palmer has to get up and pace the room. Letting out a sceptical laugh, he pushes his hands back through his blond hair and looks back at Craig. "You know what, that's just screwed up enough to be right! He was trying to settle a score – I've taken care of your problem so no need to point the finger at me!"

"Which you just did by giving the cops Jennings' name," Craig reminds him.

Letting out a long breathe, Palmer shakes his head. "Well I'm not going to lose any sleep over that. Jennings needs to be taken down – he may not have given the order to have Connor murdered, but he isn't innocent by any means!"

"Have you made any headway with the board?" Craig nods his head over to the whiteboard that Palmer has been using to compile facts surrounding Connor's death and the events leading up to it.

"Yes. I looked into that agency you spotted," Palmer tells him. "Apparently there was a man named Tom Grady, a PI with a lot of experience who worked for Connor then left the agency without giving notice." Palmer smiles, "That's why they were so cooperative in giving me the information. He really pissed them off."

"So, you think he started working for Connor full time...doin' what?" Craig frowns.

"I don't know yet. But there are regular payments to Grady from Connor's bank account so we know he was working on something for him."

Getting up, Craig walks over to the whiteboard with Palmer. "I see you've marked the payment dates and amounts," he murmurs. "What are these amounts?" he asks, pointing to some monetary amounts marked in red.

"They are Connor's mysterious incomings," Palmer clarifies. "There is no apparent rhyme or reason for them, but they are considerable."

"And he's left it all to Zoe?" Craig frowns darkly, not sure why he doesn't like the idea of that.

"Mmm. She certainly won't struggle for money – not that I would have let her," he adds distractedly. "You know, there's something about the pattern of these payments that still eludes me. It's right there, I just can't put it together."

Nodding, Craig considers them then exclaims loudly, "Fuck me! I've got it!"

"Ok, give!" Palmer tells him when Craig just stares dumbly at the figures.

"If I hadn't been workin' in the office lately, I never would have got it," Craig muses. "But I think you'll find these dates...," and he points to the dates when Connor received the large payments, "...will more or less match up to when tenders were due in — the one's you didn't win!" he explains more pointedly.

"Son of a bitch! That bloody idiot was selling off my tenders, giving someone an inside advantage!" he exclaims.

"Damn straight!"

"And these other payments, to Grady, they fall in shortly after — so he was part of the set up," Palmer surmises. "That's what he was doing for Connor. He was probably the middle man. We need to find Grady and make sure we've got this right!"

Grady had hidden himself away after he'd witnessed Connor's beating. He knew that his new boss had died and he'd laid low in case the police, or his brother had come calling.

But as nothing has happened, no mention of him on the news or in the papers, Grady takes it that no one has made the connection and that he is now free and clear.

Trouble is, the money Connor paid him is burning a hole in his pocket with no other source of income to replace it. He'll have to rectify that situation, and soon.

Grady grins to himself, wondering if he dares be cheeky enough to go back to the agency and ask for some work. He doesn't want to just live on the money Connor Johnson had paid him; where is the point in that?

So he goes back, cap in hand, to brown-nose the private investigations agency boss.

CHAPTER TWENTY-TWO

Palmer is nervous. He's found out so much about his brother's dodgy activities but he can't let Zoe know about them.

If she had any idea of the kinds of things you've been up to, it would break her heart. Damn it, Connor, couldn't you play it straight even with Zoe! You obviously cared for her!

Stretching his long lean legs as he alights his car, Palmer walks slowly up to Zoe's front door. Dressed in fitted blue-jeans and a charcoal coloured jacket with a white shirt beneath, he looks stunning and takes Zoe's breathe away when she opens the door to him.

With her heart in her mouth and her tongue almost on the floor, Zoe steps back to allow him entry.

"Not going to say, hi?" he asks with a quirk of a smile.

"I...hi," she smiles nervously, holding a hand out to indicate the front room, then dropping it quickly once she realises how much her hand is shaking.

Craig, and more especially Carly, are conspicuous in their absence. But Palmer merely raises a brow.

"Mum and Craig have gone out to dinner," Zoe explains quickly.

His smile broadens and Palmer takes a step closer. "So...we have the place to ourselves."

Zoe's breathe catches sharply as she takes a step back. "You need to behave...we're not a couple anymore. You said you wanted to talk," she babbles, and takes another step back only to feel the settee at her calf. And with an exclamation of 'oh' sits down on it with a thump.

"Now look what you did!" Zoe frowns up as Palmer begins to laugh. "It is not funny!"

But it is. She is having to roll to one side in her efforts to get back to her feet, and Palmer thinks it's hilarious.

Reaching down a hand, he makes a bid to help her up.

But instead of taking it, Zoe bats it aside exclaiming, "I can do it! I'm not a beached whale, damn it!"

But she was doing a damned good impersonation of one in Palmer's opinion.

When she finally gets to her feet, Palmer pulls her

close. "You're the sexiest thing on two legs," he tells her, his eyes darkening in appreciation of the woman in his arms.

"I..I..." Lost for words, Zoe can only stare up at him and pray that he doesn't take things further, because she is in no fit state to resist him. Her pulse is jumping all over the place, her hands itching to burrow beneath that beautifully fitted shirt. *And those jeans...damn it...they should be illegal!*

But when her prayers are answered and Palmer takes a step back, Zoe feels bereft. *No! Damn it Palmer, no!*

"Are you hungry? I got some really fine sirloin steaks and that baby corn that you like," he tells her with a huge grin.

Feeling a hunger of a very different kind, Zoe has to pull her thoughts out of the gutter fast. "That sounds great," she tells him, not even protesting that they were supposed to be eating out tonight.

"Good! Your meal awaits," he tells her, holding out his elbow as they step out the front door and begin walking down the drive. "Holding the car door open for her, Palmer rounds the bonnet and climbs in behind the wheel.

"I love you, Zoe," he pronounces as he turns in his seat. "I know you don't believe that right now, but I do," he proclaims, turning to pull his seatbelt across and buckle in. "And one day, I'm going to prove it!"

When they walk into his loft, Zoe is stunned beyond belief. There are candles of every size dotted about the dimly lit room, all glowing against the dark blue night sky.

"Palmer..." It's all she can say through the hand covering her mouth.

"Please take a seat," a waiter dressed in full regalia invites her as he holds her chair out from the beautifully set table in the middle of the huge room.

Jumping, Zoe turns to the man she hadn't even noticed, then smiles and does as she's told.

Looking down the table at Palmer as he takes his seat, Zoe lets out a nervous giggle.

"You did all this for me?"

"Of course, for you," Palmer smiles, and the love in his eyes is crystal clear. "It's all for you."

The waiter is discrete, moving to bring their starters while they gaze lovingly into each other's eyes.

"Clear vegetable soup," the waiter declares as he places a bowl in front of Zoe and then Palmer. "Would madam like a roll with that?"

"I.no...thank you," Zoe stutters nervously. She has never been waited on like this before and isn't exactly sure what's expected of her.

"They are freshly baked," the waiter informs her, then smiles when she nods her acceptance.

"This is wonderful," she exclaims after the first mouthful. "Did you cook all of this?"

Lifting his head with pride, the waiter reveals his true identity. "I am head chef and owner of my own chain of restaurants," he smiles indulgently. "I am Mr Maciejewski, but my friends call me Mac and my restaurants are-"

"The best in the world," Zoe exclaims, full of excitement. "Everyone has heard of Mr Mac! My mother and I had a meal in your restaurant three years ago to celebrate her 40th birthday!"

Bowing graciously, Mac acknowledges her compliment. "That is too long," he tells her. "You must come back and bring your beautiful mother with you," he grins impishly.

"How do you know she's beautiful?" Zoe asks, now happily confused.

"How could she not be," Mac raises a brow and takes Zoe's hand, placing a kiss on the back of it, "with a daughter as lovely as you!"

Palmer lets out a hearty laugh. "As smooth as ever, Mac," he observes, watching Zoe blush to her roots. "But accurate nevertheless."

"I will leave you to enjoy your first course while I

prepare your steaks." And Mac bows, then moves discretely away.

"He's great, isn't he," Palmer chuckles over at Zoe.

"He is, and so is his cooking. Have you tasted this," she asks him, spooning more of the clear vegetable soup into her mouth.

"He's the best. That's why he's here," Palmer smiles and watches Zoe hesitate with her spoon halfway to her mouth. "You deserve only the very best."

Blushing again, Zoe dips her head and continues to eat. She can't think of a single thing to say in reply to that!

Having cleared their dishes, Mac returns with their steaks and a beautiful array of vegetables.

"Enjoy," he tells them, then secretes himself back in the kitchen area.

"Oh. My. Lord." Zoe exclaims, the steak melting in her mouth with a flavour to die for. "I am going to be so spoiled. I'll never eat steak again after this. Nothing could live up to it!"

"He is pretty special," Palmer acknowledges. "But I think it would be a shame never to eat steak again. Didn't you enjoy it when we cooked our own steak?"

Remembering back to those intimate dinners they'd shared, Zoe feels a veil of sadness creep over her. *I miss those times more than I should, and much more than I want to!*

Then she becomes aware of the music swirling around them in the background. It is one of her favourite artists, Eva Cassidy singing Over the Rainbow.

"Stop over thinking this," Palmer tells her, seeing the shadows falling over her expression.

Trying to pull herself out of the doldrums, Zoe gives him her best smile. "You're right – this is such a special treat. Thank you, Palmer, I am enjoying this."

But you feel guilty for doing so. I know you well enough to realise that. But you're wrong, it's ok to be happy, you don't need to feel guilty about that. Even Connor wouldn't begrudge you a life after his death!

With the meal over and Mac having taken his leave, they sit on the settee listening to the last strains of the Eva Cassidy album.

"I love her music," Zoe tells him, though the way she is looking at Palmer gives his heart a twist.

"I love you, Zoe," he tells her softly, his fingers trailing up and down her arm.

A second Eva Cassidy album has kicked in and the candlelight and soulful music are playing on Zoe's senses.

"Palmer..."

His eyes never leave hers as his lips descend, his hand moving up her arm and to the back of her neck.

No. We shouldn't. We can't. Please...Palmer...don't stop...

The night is still and the room dark when Zoe wakes a few hours later. Naked in Palmer's bed, she draws back the quilt and moves to the floor to ceiling windows.

For a long time she stands looking out at the Birmingham skyline, the moon glinting silver off the windows of neighbouring buildings.

But the beauty of Palmer's loft is that it is not overlooked. She can stand in all her glory without fear of being seen.

"You look beautiful," Palmer tells her, walking up to Zoe and sliding his arms around her to lay his hands on her swollen belly. "Jesus! Was that Brook? Did she just kick my hand?!"

Smiling up at him Zoe nods, her long auburn hair falling forward over her bare breasts.

"She gets restless at night," Zoe tells him.

"Like her mother," Palmer smiles, his hands massaging her stomach lovingly.

"I've always found this liberating," she tells him, wafting a hand to encompass the openness of their situation. "No neighbours, no curtains, and no need to get dressed. I suppose it's kind of kinky, but I love that I can stand here naked and look out on the world."

"If they only knew," he grins, then draws her hair back and dips his head to kiss her neck.

Her small groan is like electricity along his veins, shimmering into him and through him down to his groin.

His lips move to her ear, nibbling, tasting, licking and probing, until she turns in his arms and claims those expert lips.

Her tongue probes his mouth, taking, demanding, the kiss so full of need.

And he gives willingly, softly, then furiously. His woman is back in his arms where she belongs, back in his life where he is determined to keep her.

Crouching to take her sensitive nipple into his mouth, his hand cups her other breast as his thumb strums her nipple.

Zoe gasps, his twin assault almost causing her knees to buckle under her. Dropping a hand to the back of her knees, Palmer scoops her up and takes her back to his bed where he loves her long and hard.

They have always been an intimately physical couple, their bodies so in tune to each other, their responses immediate and overwhelming.

When his tongue finds her sex, Zoe screams his name into the darkness, her body jerking uncontrollably.

"Please...Palmer...oh god!"

She doesn't need to beg, but he loves how much he can make her want him. He is harder than he's ever known himself to be, such is his need of this woman who is carrying his child.

"Zoe, you drive me crazy!" And rearing up in front of her, he lifts her hips and thrusts deep inside of her.

Her scream of passion is empowering, his thrusts deeper and harder, his words endearing and suggestive at the same time.

"So beautiful! So sexy and so damned beautiful!"

Zoe lifts her hips to him, meeting him thrust for thrust and beat for heavenly beat.

"Palmer!" When she screams his name for the last time he can feel her orgasm rip through her and drag him over the top.

"I love you. I love you. I. Love. You," he tells her, emphasising his words with ever deeper thrusts.

When their vision is lost, when the world disappears around them, they fall slowly into each other and the happy oblivion that good sex brings.

EPILOGUE

Sneaking out of Palmer's loft had taken all of Zoe's resolve. Lying with him in his bed had been so natural, so much what she wanted that it had frightened her.

The note she had left on her pillow for Palmer had been short and to the point.

'I can't do this, Palmer. Without trust love can't survive, and without love sex is meaningless. That isn't how I want to remember us, Palmer. Please don't follow. I need time to get over losing Connor, and to get over losing you again, too. I know it's my own fault, but loving you has always been so easy for me – it seems falling out of love is that much harder. I wish you happiness in your life, Palmer, and hope that one day we can be friends. For now, I'll say goodbye and God Bless, yours, Zoe.'

Her mother had pleaded with her to stay, to give it more time, but Zoe had been adamant.

The long train journey is just what Zoe needs. Sitting by the window she leans against it, allowing the hot tears to fall.

Alone again, her head in turmoil and her heart in tatters, Zoe has to draw a line under the past and move on to her future.

With her father's help she will provide a stable home for her daughter. Something she could never do with Palmer in her life.

How could I have stayed? It would never have worked! The trust is gone. If only I could say the same for our love!

He really seemed to care. The lengths he went to, to convince me, were extreme to say the least. That meal was wonderful, and Mac was such a character.

Her tears continue to fall as Zoe watches the miles pass her by.

She feels Brook move in her womb and hugs her arms around her rounded stomach.

"It's alright, baby," she whispers softly. "Mummy's here. We'll be alright, we have each other." *That will have to be enough!*

The cottage is cold but welcoming when Zoe steps

through the door. Moving to the kitchen she fills the kettle and plugs it in to boil.

Sitting at the kitchen table, Zoe looks around her, taking in her lonely surroundings.

You need to toughen up. You have a child to support and a new life to build. What good will it do to cry...absolutely none at all!

But the tears fall anyway. With her arms folded on the table she leans her forehead onto them and sobs.

Connor will never again walk through the door; will never again tell her that all will be well; she is truly on her own again.

I'm so sorry, Connor. Sorry that I couldn't love you, and so sorry to have lost you. No one understands how kind and gentle you really were. No one but me, and I will never forget you, Connor. Not ever!

*****

If you have enjoyed this book, please leave a review at the place from where you purchased it. Thank you.